DARK
WATERS

DALE DRAKE

For Nanny May and the good people of Mevagissey.

Nemo me impune lacessit

ACKNOWLEDGEMENTS

Cover picture by Matthew Facey

www.facebook.com/MevagisseyPhoto

The characters and situations in this book are entirely imaginary and bear no relation to any real person or happenings.

CONTENTS

Chapel Point

Feast Week

Vandraven

Clotted Cream

The Dressmaker's Dummy

The Well

Joe's Tale

Seated

Broken Messiah

CHAPEL POINT

Chapel Point. The name dragged Tom's attention away from the article he was reading in the local paper, something about the decline of the British bee population. For some reason, the name sounded familiar. He looked up to see from what direction the name had come and spotted two old timers sat by the fire as they whispered in the conspiratory tones of the terminally deaf.

"It was in all the local papers," the one with his back to Tom continued. "Threw herself off the rocks at Chapel Point, she did."

Tom unconsciously leaned a little closer, struggling with the local accent. He had only moved to Cornwall a couple of weeks ago and the local dialect, like the local people, were a complete fucking mystery to him.

"Left a note, did she?" the other man asked.

"Aye, she did. Found her body before they found any note, though! Been in the water two days before she washed up on Polstreath beach. Crabs had been at her," he said, taking a long pull on his pint. "All chewed up she was. At least that's what my cousin, Andy, says."

"There, was he?"

"Aye, course he was, had to be being the local constable and all, had to go down the steps. Him and two coroners carrying a stretcher two hundred steps down to that beach with the wind howling and sea spray half blinding them. Pure luck one of 'em didn't fall and break a leg or worse. You know them old metal steps, rickety and slippery as the devil they are." The other man nodded and suddenly glanced up, looking Tom straight in the eye. Tom, embarrassed at being caught eavesdropping, immediately raised his paper and pretended to scan the stories. The paper was suddenly snatched from his grasp by a gnarled hand.

"Page two," the old man snarled, slamming the paper back down on the table hard enough to make Tom's glass tremble. "Ain't no secret, boy, not here, not in this village." That said, he shoved his hands roughly in his pockets and stalked off, mumbling and slamming the pub door behind him. The other man stood up and ambled over to Tom.

"Sorry about that, young fella. David Parsons always had a quick temper. Bad business that," he said, nodding to Tom's paper which now lay open on page two, the black and white picture of a young girl smiling up at him from between the pages.

"Listen," Tom began, "I didn't mean to offend your friend." The other man waved it away and sat down.

"You never mind old David. Like I said, always had a quick temper on him and an even quicker tongue. Damn shame about young missy, though," he said, tapping the photo with one nicotine stained finger. "Lovely girl, she was. Daughter of Jim and Amanda who own the bakery."

Tom had only been in the bakery a couple of times since he moved to the village and had trouble putting the names to the faces. Tom looked at the photo again. The girl had been a real beauty with a vivacious smile. A girl that seemed to have everything to live for.

"Any idea why she did it? Did she leave a note or anything?" Tom asked.

"Well," the old man said, drawing near and lowering his voice to a conspiratory whisper. It was all Tom could do not to flinch away from his beer soaked breath. "My cousin Andy is the local constable here about and he told me she did it. Wasn't much of a note. They found it pinned to a branch, said how she was tired of life that's all, nothing else. I tell yah, young fella," he said, taking out his pipe and beginning to fill it with fragrant tobacco. "There must be a lot of tired people here and about these days."

"What do you mean?" Tom asked, intrigued, perhaps sensing some kind of story here, perhaps even a mystery.

"All this talking is thirsty work," the old man said, licking his lips and eyeing Tom's pint appreciatively. "Think I will step outside and have myself a pipe. When I come back, maybe we will talk some more. Name's Joe, by the way."

"Tom," Tom said, holding out his hand. The hand was taken and pumped twice in a hand surprisingly strong for one so old.

"Mine is a pint of bitter."

"What makes you think I am buying?" Tom said, smiling back.

"What a writer fella like you," the old man laughed at Tom's surprised expression. "Never met a writer fella who didn't like a good yarn."

"Met many writers have you?"

"One or two in my tangier," the old man laughed. "The only thing down here thicker than tourists is painters and writers. And the only thing thicker then all three are our pasties." Chuckling to himself, he turned and headed for the door.

Five minutes later, the old party was back, smelling of bitter pipe smoke, a smell Tom found rather pleasant, almost comforting. His father had smoked a pipe and he'd always liked the smell.

"So," he said, handing old Joe his beer. "You said you had a story." The old man took a big drink before wiping the foam off his lip and eyeing Tom shrewdly.

"Aye, a story in a way. A little local history and if you're thinking of settling down in these parts, perhaps even a warning!"

"A warning?" Tom said, turning more fully to face the other man. "What kind of warning?"

"Best to let me tell it in the right order first," the old man said, holding up a restraining hand, "or you won't understand. Let me start by telling you this: there have been over forty suicides at Chapel Point in the last twenty years." Tom's mouth literally dropped open. He knew he was gawping like an idiot but he couldn't seem to help himself.

"Forty?" he whispered.

"Aye," Joe nodded. "May not seem so much if you was in one of those great big cities like they have over there in America. I heard hundreds of people throw themselves off of that Golden Gate Bridge alone. But forty is a hell of a lot for a small rural place like this that numbers about three thousand residents all year round. Well, until the summer people come, of course, with their caravans and noisy motor boats! Want to know something even stranger?" Tom nodded numbly. "They all left a note, all pinned to the same tree overlooking the drop. And pretty much all saying the same thing. They was tired of living, or something along the same vein. Some thought there was some kind of foul play going on and even sent for some big city detective from somewhere up country to take a look at one of the bodies."

"And what did he find?" Tom asked, his mouth dry.

"Nothing," Joe shrugged. "Death by blunt trauma and drowning. My cousin Andy was new on the job back then but he told me that big city detective found a few things he weren't too happy with. Something about strange marks on the body. But Michael Clutterbuck, the local coroner, set him to rights, told him how the body had been in the water two days, bashed about on rocks and picked at by fish and crabs, maybe even hit by a fishing boat propeller or two. No wonder it was in such a state. Well that detective left but he was apparently none too happy with the outcome. Took some photos of the body and off he went, never to be seen again. And the suicides went on and on."

"All local people?" Tom asked.

"Mostly," the old man said, drinking the dregs of his pint. "Local or here about, although a couple of times it's been summer people. Was a man a few years back down from York, I think it was, on a camping holiday with his family, went for a walk in the evening along the coastal path from here to Pentewan."

"That's where it is?" Tom interrupted. "This Chapel Point between here and Pentewan?"

"Aye," the old man, nodded. "That's where that fella went and never come back. They found a note, same as all the others, and a few days later what was left of him washed up on Polstreath Beach, just like the rest. So now you know why the locals don't walk along the coastal path to Pentewan no more or frequent Polstreath Beach. Some say it's cursed, others haunted by dead smugglers. Crazy Maureen, who runs the crystal shop and reads tarot cards in the local pub when she's had a few rums, even says it's magnetism, just like the Bermuda Triangle," he cackled.

"And you?" Tom asked, finishing his drink. "What do you think it is?"

"Fairies," the old man laughed. "Got to be fairies. Now how about another drink?"

Tom woke the next day with an aching head and a mouth dry as old bark. He had stayed in the pub right up till closing time, pumping old Joe for information, although there wasn't much more to tell. Forty suicides in all, men, women and even a few teenage kids. All left a note stuck to the same tree like some kind of weird ritual then jumped to their deaths on the rocks and into the raging seas below. What was left of them washed up on Polstreath Beach a few days later, something Tom had found strange until Joe had told him about the rip tides and currents that swirled and ebbed just off the shores of the deserted beach.

He had staggered home that night to his rented accommodation and passed out fully dressed on his bed. Now, after a shower and a quick breakfast of eggs, toast and a couple of cups of strong black coffee, he felt ready to face the world again. All he needed was a breath of fresh air and Tom knew exactly where to get it.

The entrance to the coastal path was just where old Joe had said it would be at the end of Beach Road, just passed the last house on the left. Tom noted, with some trepidation, that the house was boarded up, its garden overgrown and its paint peeling. This was in stark contrast to the rest of the houses that Tom had passed as he walked down the street. The area was obviously one of affluence, the houses large and detached, with large bay windows that overlooked the sea. There was a car or an SUV in every drive and the gardens were all well-kept and maintained, all except this one. Tom suppressed a shudder. Suddenly the day felt colder and he had to rub his arms to stop the goose flesh from rising there.

Giving himself a mental shake, he turned and looked at the overgrown path before him. Old Joe had told him how the village council had stopped maintaining the path a few years back and had asked the local shops and business owners not to mention the path or the hidden beach to the summer people for fear of anymore incidents. In that time, the entrance to the path had become overgrown with small trees and thorny brambles that had come together to form a kind of tunnel. The surrounding ground was knee high with blackberry brambles and a good healthy crop of this year's nettles. Tom was regretting his choice of shorts already but there was a story here, damn it. He could feel it in his bones. Just like the old days, all he needed was one more story to complete his anthology of weird tales. He was already over his deadline by two months and his publisher at Black Days was on the phone breaking his balls with a constant litany of "is the book ready yet, is the book ready yet?" until Tom felt like he could scream. That's why he had left Manchester behind, and hopefully the writer's block with it, and come here to this tranquil part of the Cornish coast.

He had been here less than two weeks and already this story had fallen into his lap. All he needed was to get a feel for the place, to see this Chapel Point with his own eyes, to soak up the atmosphere and then write all about it and get the damn book finished, head back to the big city, pick up his cheque and relax. All these thoughts went through his mind in a matter of seconds as he hitched up his shorts, took a deep breath and stepped onto the path that led to Chapel Point.

The path along the cliff tops was nothing like what Tom was expecting. It was actually very pretty with amazing views of the ocean. Wild flowers grew along the sides of the path, attracting butterflies and honey bees. Here and there, the view was blocked by small trees that grew slanted along the cliff's edge, their branches causing dappled patterns where the sunlight shone through onto the dirt path that Tom now walked along. Everywhere was the sound of birds and the gentle lap of waves below.

He walked for a further ten minutes, soaking in the beauty of the place, before he came across the wooden steps that led down to Polstreath Beach. He paused, losing some of the bounce from his step. There was something in the air, here. A certain sense of foreboding perhaps or perhaps it was just the path that led down to the beach. It was dark in there and the trees had become overgrown, forming a kind of dark tunnel. The steps were wet looking and splintered. Pale looking fungus and moss grew on the sides of the damp trees whose rough bark was encrusted here and there with salt from the ocean and a goodish collection of last autumn's leaves lay strewn about giving off their musty odour. The scene was one of neglect and foreboding. Tom had planned to go down and check out the beach but old Joe had told him the wooden steps went on for some time before giving way to the newer metal stairs.

Well, Tom had decided he didn't want to spend any time in there, not today, not with the weather being so fine and quickly moved on.

Five minutes later, he rounded a bend and got his first glimpse of Chapel Point. The point was no more than an extension of the cliff face, a flattened spur that jutted out over the ocean. The old man had told him the place was named after an old chapel that had been built there sometime in the distant past. If such a place ever did exist, there was no sign of it now, only waving sea grass and one small skeletal looking tree that seemed to cling to the edge of the crumbling cliff with a kind of desperate intensity. The only signs of man's intervention on the rugged terrain were the stone steps that had been chiselled into the very rock face itself. Tom counted thirty leading down onto the windswept plateau. He also noted that there was no guard rail and knew he would never have the guts to make such a perilous descent. He did, however, want to see the point from both sides before heading back, maybe even get a few pictures on his phone as a memento, a little inspiration to take back home. Hurriedly, he carried on up the path which now started to incline sharply. There was a high hill that directly overlooked the point. From here, he would be able to see the shape of the plateau more clearly and maybe see the rocks that waited below.

Twenty minutes later, breathing hard but feeling good nevertheless, he stood atop the hill. To his left, in the far distance, he could just make out the gabled roofs and spires of Pentewan, behind him, nothing but farmer's fields, and, to his right, Chapel Point. His first assessment had been right. The point was just that, a lump of rock shaped like an arrow pointing out into the cold seas of the Atlantic Ocean. Some hundred or so feet below was a long sharp hunk of barnacle covered reef that jutted out of the ocean like the spine of some long dead sea beast or maybe one of Lovecraft's dreaming elder gods.

Tom pulled out his phone and began snapping away, trying to catch as many angles as he could. When he was finished, he pocketed his phone and headed back down. He had only taken a few steps, when he turned back round, meaning to get a picture of Pentewan. That's when he saw the woman.

For a minute, he stood there transfixed. The woman had literally appeared from nowhere. Thoughts of ghosts flashed through his mind but the woman seemed solid enough. She was wearing a green summer dress and flat sensible shoes but it was the old fashioned gloves that caught his attention. They were straight out of the twenties, long white silk that covered the forearm and stopped just before the elbow. The hat was of the same style and colour, only netted somewhat obscuring the woman's face. In her gloved hand, she held some kind of paper pad and seemed to be writing or perhaps sketching.

Tom let out a breath he didn't realise he had been holding and quickly turned away and headed back down, calling himself all kinds of fool. The woman had simply been in dead ground, he told himself, and he had been too busy snapping away to notice her approach, that was all. And yet, something didn't ring true. He had had a completely unobstructed view of the surrounding countryside and there had been no one around, absolutely no one. "Perhaps she came from the sea," he laughed then stopped.

Suddenly, the hair on the back of his neck started to rise and the skin on his arms had begun to crawl. He spun around and the woman was there about thirty feet behind him, standing on the top step, looking directly at him from behind large black sunglasses. She didn't move but stood completely motionless and Tom was forcefully reminded of a game they used to play as kids, Postman's Knock, where one kid turned his back and the rest crept up on him until he would spin round, trying his best to catch them in the act.

He actually took a step forward, meaning to speak when the smell assailed him, the smell of long dead oceans, of rotting fish and bloated waterlogged corpses. Gagging, he retched and staggered away, half falling and sliding down the hill. He risked a look back. But the woman was gone. Now the day seemed darker, the sound of the crashing surf down below wilder. The wind had picked up, rippling his clothes. There was a sense of danger all about him and Tom realised he was afraid, in fact it was so much more than that. It was terror, abject terror.

His entire body was taut. His flesh seemed to be crawling all over his body and the hair on his head felt stiff and brittle.

With a cry, he bolted, running in a blind panic back the way he had come but the wind seemed to push at him, as if forcing him backwards, trying to hinder his escape as the sea below crashed and howled like a mad man's laughter. As he blundered past the stairs that led to Chapel Point, he suddenly tripped and fell face first into the dirt, crushing his nose and scratching his face. Blood was running freely down his shirt now but, in his terror, Tom felt nothing as he scrambled to his feet. And then she was suddenly there, blocking his escape. Tom let out a scream as she drew closer, reaching out with gloved hands. With a cry, he stumbled backwards, missing his footing, his arms pin-wheeling for balance. The woman smiled then shoved him hard in the chest, sending him flying down the stairs that led to Chapel Point. He crashed down hard, feeling something snap in his side as he cartwheeled down, landing in a bloody heap.

At the bottom, he climbed to his knees then staggered to his feet. He could hear her coming now, eagerly hurrying down the steps behind him. Gasping and holding his side, he lurched blindly onwards then suddenly stopped. There was nowhere left to go. The cliff abruptly ended, falling away to the jagged rocks a hundred feet below. The ground under his feet started to shift and crumble. With a cry, almost instinctively, he reached out and grabbed the small stunted tree at his side and suddenly he understood everything. This was the tree and this was the place. Not a place of suicide but a hunting ground.

Slowly he turned, just as she was finishing her note, his note now. She tore the paper from the pad and let it slip from her fingers. Flying, defying the wind, it floated straight towards his face then veered sharply to the right, impaling itself on the branch closest to him. He turned his head, as if in a dream, and read the note. It said how he was tired of life and tired of his failure to finish his latest book. The note was even signed. The signature on the bottom of the note wasn't a copy of his signature. It was his signature.

He turned in the deadly slowness of nightmares, just as green leprous tentacles burst forth from the creature's gloved hands. The dark glasses melted away, leaving black pupil-less eyes, cold and soulless. The hat and dress melted into a scaly, crooked body that was covered in a cold noxious smelling slime. Tom let out a scream as those terrible arms engulfed him and suddenly he was falling through the air, the cold wind rushing past his face, before plunging into the freezing depths below. Then nothing.

He awoke sometime later in the dripping darkness. He had time for one scream before it began to feed.

Above, the wind howled and screamed like a siren's song around Chapel Point.

FEAST WEEK

Michael Mason had just taken his drink from the bar and found himself a comfortable seat by the window when the girl entered the pub. The smell of incense and the sound of revelry from outside suddenly swelled and then was just as quickly cut short as the door swung closed behind her. The girl was a real looker: blonde, small, petite with curves in all the right places. Michael felt a stirring of lust that was almost vicious in its intensity and quickly looked away as the girl swept past, heading for the bar, leaving behind her a trail of sweet smelling perfuming. Michael sighed, breathing the girl in, and felt depression drop over him like an unwanted shadow. How long had it been since he had been with a woman? He and Steph had split up over six months ago and there had been no other woman since.

Michael gave himself a mental shake and reached for his bag, no point dwelling on the past, not now when he was so close to completing the new book. Reaching inside, he pulled out his notes and laid them out across the table before picking one out at random and started to read.

The file was written in his own clumsy script and detailed the myth and legends surrounding the old druid kings of Britain, their rituals and sacrificial practices, both before and after the Roman occupation. Sighing, he picked up another file and flipped it open. This one was a written account of

Stonehenge categorising archaeological finds and druid type burials in and around the Salisbury area.

With a sigh, he let the file fall back onto the table then swept the whole damn lot back into his bag, before staring moodily out of the window. The notes, the Goddamn notes. There had been a book there once. Hell, there still was, just not the same book he had originally wanted to write. Originally the book, his second, had started out as a work of fiction, a sprawling saga with druid kings, a defeated Roman army and an ailing emperor, all set in the mist shrouded valleys and forests of ancient Britain. But, somewhere along the line, it had all started to change. The research had become more interesting than the actual book. Michael found himself becoming intrigued by the old myths and Celtic legends. Tales of druids and their foul rights, as chronicled by Julius Caesar in his Commentarii de Bello Gallico, and later by such writers and noblemen as Cicero Tactus and Pliny the Elder. It was this research, this growing obsession that had brought him here to Mevagissey on the Cornish coast to observe and document the ancient festival of Feast Week, a festival that had its roots firmly planted into the distant past.

He had first heard of Mevagissey whilst visiting the ancient ruin of Tintagel. The carpark had a small café nearby, a tourist hotspot where visitors could go get a bite to eat or a hot drink to fortify themselves against the rainy British weather. It was here, while sipping tea and munching on a biscuit, that he noticed a small wooden bookcase laden with pamphlets of all different shapes and sizes. Finishing his tea, he stood up, fastened his coat and left, almost as an afterthought picking up a few random pamphlets as he passed on his way out the door. It was only later, after the long drive to Newquay as he lay down in his hotel room that he actually bothered to look at what he had picked up.

The first pamphlet was a flyer for Sea World in Plymouth, another for a kids' place called Farming Fun and the last was a flyer advertising Mevagissey Feast Week. This finally piqued Mike's interest and he sat up straighter in bed, resting his head against the headboard as he read. According to the pamphlet, Feast Week was an ancient Mevagissey tradition going back to hallowed antiquity and believed to be one of the forefathers of the Christian harvest festival. It was a time of celebration, to thank the land and Mother Sea for her bountiful harvest.

Over the course of a week, the people of Mevagissey would have raft races in the local harbour, bands and choirs would perform, open air markets, drink and food tents would be erected and the children from the local school would take part in a floral dance to thank Mother Earth. The week's festivities would end with what the locals called the Fish Festival, a lantern lit parade that ran through the streets of Mevagissey. Here, the local fishermen would hoist a raft upon their shoulders, attached a paper lit figure of a virgin maid clasping a fish to her bosom. Through the darkened streets of Mevagissey, they slowly made their way. Behind them the local people would follow with homemade lanterns, some banging drums and others ringing small bells until the procession would stop at the harbour front. Here, they would place the raft gently into the sea, a man would come forward, usually the harbour master, give thanks to the ocean for her great bounty and then, to rapturous applause, he would set the effigy on fire before floating it out into the night shrouded ocean.

The whole thing reeked of paganism and Mike was hooked and knew he would have to see it for himself.

His musing was suddenly interrupted by a polite cough. It was the girl from the bar. She was standing above him, one eyebrow raised quizzically. He swallowed hard, realising she had spoken, as he sat lost in his own thoughts, and was waiting for a reply. Feeling like a fool, Mike coughed embarrassedly.

"Sorry," he said, with a nervous smile. "I was away with the fairies."

"The fairies," she smiled. "You're in the right place. My grandmother used to swear there were fairies in the local wood, even at the bottom of our garden living amongst the rhubarb patch." Michael smiled back. He found her voice soothing and liked the way her Cornish accent added a certain lilt to her words. "I am Autumn," the girl said, holding out a slender hand. Michael took the offered hand and marvelled at how soft the skin felt beneath his own.

"I am Michael, Michael Mason."

"May I sit?" the girl asked, indicating the chair across from him with one slender arm.

"Yes," Michael said, feeling a small sweat break out beneath his collar. She really was beautiful, almost intoxicating. Her only flaw was her eyes. They were dark in contrast to the paleness of her skin and the blondness of her hair but, for Michael, this only enhanced her beauty, adding a certain smouldering sexuality. Again, he felt that familiar stirring of lust and tried not to look at the perfection of her throat or the swell of her breast as she sat down, placing her drink between them.

"I hope I am not bothering you," she said, playing with the stem of her wine glass, "but I was expecting a friend. She never showed and I hate to drink alone. Michael quickly surveyed the room, seeing all the other men, some in groups, others alone. The girl laughed as if reading his mind. "What, them?" she said, quickly glancing over her shoulder before turning back. "I know almost every man in this room, well local men, anyway, and do you know what they are?" When Michael didn't reply she went on, "they're fishermen and farmers. Now, don't get me wrong, nothing wrong with being either a fisherman or farmer but there are only so many conversations a girl can have about tractors and fishing nets." Michael couldn't help but laugh.

"Probably doesn't make for stimulating conversation, now does it."

"Well," she said, arching one perfectly sculpted eyebrow, "it's ok for the first twenty or thirty times." At this, Michael burst out laughing, drawing some sullen looks from the men around the room and some envious ones he fancied too. "Why are you here?" the girl asked, slowly sipping her drink. Michael tried not to watch as her bow shaped lips pressed against the rim of her glass, leaving a faint trace of lipstick behind.

"Don't many people come here," he replied, "especially at this time of year?"

"Yes, but not as many as in summer. It's near autumn time now, the time of the harvest. Some of the people you see out there," she said, indicating towards the window, "are tourists come to watch the festival but most of them are locals from the village or the surrounding farms and homesteads. They know that for the village the time of the harvest is upon us tonight. Tomorrow, with its gaudy fireworks and frilly display, is for the tourists and tourists alone. But forget about us. Tell me more about you. Why are you here and are you here by yourself?" He tried not to think about the second question or read too much into it. Nevertheless, his palms felt somewhat damp as he drained the last dregs of his pint.

"I am here doing research."

"Another writer," she grinned. Michael smiled back, somewhat whimsically.

"Guess you see many writers down this way."

"Yes," she replied, "writers, singers, painters and even a movie maker or two. There is something in the air that seems to bring out the muse in people, that and the gorgeous scenery. So tell me, what are you writing about?" Usually Michael didn't discuss his work but he couldn't imagine himself denying this girl anything for long!

"It's a factual piece about the ancient Celtic religions, their druid leaders and kings," he said, playing with his empty glass.

"Really?" the girl said, cocking her head coquettishly to one side.

"Yes, also about their rituals and celebrations."

"And that's why you came here? To watch the Fish Festival and lantern parade?"

"Yes, do you know much about them?" The girl looked at her watch.

"It's getting late," she said, looking out the window at the dwindling revellers outside. "I could tell you what I know," she went on, "but, like I said, it's getting late and if you have someone waiting for you at wherever you're staying they may start to get worried about you."

"No fear of that," he said, looking quietly. "I am here alone."

"Then perhaps you would like to ring someone back home before it gets too late? You know how people worry about loved ones, especially when they're away." Michael laughed.

"Not to worry," Michael said. "I have no family to speak of, not even a brother or sister, all alone in the big bad world," he chuckled.

"That's good," the girl smiled, reaching across the table, taking his hand before squeezing it gently. "I'll go to the bar and get us some drinks then we will talk," and with a swish of her skirt she was gone.

Michael couldn't help but watch her go, admiring the length of her leg and the roundness of her calf. He also noticed how empty the bar had become. Only a few bearded fellows sat in a corner drinking the local brew and chatting quietly amongst themselves. Even the bartender had changed to a big gruff looking man who dwarfed the girl where she stood in his shadow ordering their drinks. He had just pulled out a pad and pen when the girl came back, a drink in each hand. She sat back down and handed him his drink.

"A local brew," she smiled, "endorsed by Mevagissey royalty since 1888."

"Mevagissey royalty?"

"The fisherman," she laughed. "Didn't you know all fisherman are royalty in a fishing village? Some of these families have been fishing here for four hundred years."

"Really?" Michael said, picking up his pen and making a quick note. "You said you would tell me about the Fish Festival," he continued, turning to a fresh page. Laughing, she gently brushed his pen to one side and closed his note book.

"Make your notes later," she smiled. "I like to have a man's full attention when I speak, and drink your drink. It's as much a part of history round here as anything else." Michael did as he was bid, taking a long pull from his pint. The ale was smooth and golden but held a bitter undertone that Michael found slightly unpleasant.

"So, the Fish Festival," Michael pushed gently. The girl sighed somewhat whimsically.

"I can't say I know much more than anyone else. Jenny Starcher, who owns the local book store, would know more than me. She is a local historian and even wrote a book on the place." Michael made a quick note then took another sip of his pint. The beer was actually quite good and he suddenly found himself very thirsty. He put the glass down then picked it straight back up and took another long drink. As he put it back down, he was surprised to see over half of it was already gone.

"Told you, you would like it," Autumn said, taking a small sip from her own glass.

"It grows on you," Michael nodded. The room had started to spin ever so slightly. He squinted at the clock and saw that it was ten past midnight. Outside, the streets had become quiet and deserted. Shaking his head, he took a deep breath and tried to concentrate. Apparently, the local brew was stronger than he thought and he decided to slow down and take it easy or he would have one hell of a hangover in the morning.

"So, the Fish Festival," she went on, "just like the sea it seems like it has been a part of the village forever. I used to do the floral dance as a little girl. I remember always being terrified when they drowned the maid."

"Drowned the maid?" he asked and was surprised to hear a slight slur in his voice.

"Yes, it marks the end of the festival." Yes, Michael remembered reading something about that which started roughly a thousand years ago. Suddenly, his head was swimming and he found it hard to concentrate. "My grandfather and his father's father all participated in the drowning of the maid. In the old days, a great figurine was made out of old lobsterpots and fishing nets. In those dim dark days, the belly of the maid was filled with chickens, rabbits and all sorts of things before being burned, a blood sacrifice to thank the goddess for the sea's great bounty and to ensure the success of the next year's harvest."

"The goddess," Michael slurred. Suddenly, his whole body felt heavy. He tried to raise his hand but could not move.

"Yes, the goddess," she said, leaning closer until their lips were nearly touching. "The goddess always demands sacrifice."

The last thing he remembered before the darkness drew him under was the softness of her lips upon his own.

He awoke sometime later, a great lethargy had settled into his bones and he was hardly able to move as two burley fishermen who held both his arms dragged him outside onto the harbour where now the entire village awaited his arrival. They had formed a half circle round a giant maiden. Her body was made from barnacle covered lobster pots and seaweed covered netting. Her swollen belly was open, forming a giant cage, where she floated moored to the harbour side.

Suddenly, Michael understood everything. He tried to struggle against the effects of the drug but the fishermen tightened their grip and propelled him forward. Four figures stepped out of the shadows. One of them was Autumn, now dressed in a robe of purest white. She held a large scallop shell in her hands, engraved with intricate designs. Her companions were all men dressed in similar garb: one held a large fish, freshly caught from the ocean, its blood smeared his flawless gown, the other man held a large crab, alive, its claws tied shut by foul smelling seaweed and the last man wore a crown made of seaweed, shells and drift wood. It was this man who started the chanting. As Michael was dragged forward, the villagers of Mevagissey closed in about him, their homemade lanterns raised drums sounded somewhere in the crowd.

As he was forced down upon his knees, the priest with the fish came forward and slit its belly, its blood and guts pouring into Michael's upturned face. He tried to scream, to shout his outrage, but still was unable to move. The second priest joined the first and unwove the crab's claws, thrusting it forward into Michael's face, letting it tear at his flesh. And then she was there before him. Kneeling down, she placed the scallop shell in his shirt.

"For your journey," she whispered. "Don't be afraid, Michael. The goddess will embrace you and the darkness of the ocean shall smother the flames. You shall be reborn in the darkened womb of the great mother and bring prosperity to her most humble servants." That said, she placed a chaste kiss upon his bloody brow and stepped away.

A shadow fell over him as the high priest stood before him. Still chanting in a ringing voice, the priest removed the crown from his own head and gently placed it upon Michael's brow. Then, with a wave of his hand, indicated to the two fishermen who dragged him to his feet and thrust him inside the waiting maiden, slamming and locking the cage door behind him, sending him sprawling onto a bed of foul smelling seaweed.

The high priest stopped his chanting and raised his arms for silence.

"On this sacred day," he intoned, "we give sacrifices to our Mother Sea for her great bounty, which she has bestowed upon us, and with humble heart offer these scarifies to curry her favour for the coming months ahead. May she bless us with her harvest."

"May she bless us!" the crowed replied. A flaming torch was brought forward and handed to the priest. One of the fishermen that had held Michael's arm quickly knelt down and let loose the rope that held the maiden to her mooring. Michael felt the maiden begin to bob on the calm waters of the harbour and managed to struggle to his knees, just in time to see the high priest thrust his flaming torch into the dried seaweed and driftwood piled about the maiden's feet. Instantly, the seaweed combusted into flames and the smell of petroleum filled the air. From the harbour side, the fishermen came forward and, with long poles, pushed the now flaming maiden away from the harbour and onto the still waters.

Inside the maiden, Michael Mason began to scream as the first flames licked at his body. He tried to climb, to twist away but even as the fire started eating through his skin, he was unable to move. The last thing he heard before the smoke sent him into merciful oblivion was the sound of chanting that swept across the night darkened waters of Mevagissey harbour.

VANDRAVEN

November 1836

Finally, it's done. I have sold my half of Vandraven & Morrison to my old partner, and friend, Robert Morrison. He is now the proud owner of twenty of the finest clipper ships to ever sail from Southampton. May they serve him well in his future endeavours! As for myself, I am content. My new wife is young, beautiful and the daughter of a wealthy planter well established in the Jamaicas. Her heritage is old, almost as old as my own, if not quite as prestigious. Accompanying her is her maid, Matilda, a wild creature of mixed heritage, a dusky beauty indeed who never leaves my wife's side. I believe my man servant, Stevens, is already in love! We count ourselves lucky to have such gracious company as we undertake the long voyage back to England.

December 1836

The new house is a marvel. Sat atop a rearing cliff, it overlooks the dark waters of the Atlantic in the picturesque village of Mevagissey, which sits nestled on the southern coast of windswept Cornwall. On our arrival, we were greeted by Jonathan Wills, builder and architect, who I had at some expense commissioned to build the house. After some pleasant trivialities, he took me gently to one side and explained to me some of the extra cost I had incurred during my long absence. Most of these seemed to revolve around compensatory like matters as two workers, both men from the village, had died whilst working on the house. One had died after falling from the scaffolding and the other crushed to death by falling masonry from faulty rigging. I enquired of Wills how this was any concern of mine, after all the men had been hired legally and paid an honest day's wage for an honest day's labour. Any misfortune that had befallen them through accident, act of God or their own carelessness was no concern of mine.

It was at this point that I first learned of the villagers' dislike of not only myself but also that of my new home. Wills informed me, in no uncertain terms, that it would be in my best interest, and a gesture of goodwill, if I was to compensate the grieving widows of both men. After some little thought, I agreed on the condition that he tell me what grievances the village and its denizens held against myself and my new home. He agreed and commenced with the telling of his tale.

According to Wills, the ground upon which my new house stood was considered by many of the villagers, and others here and about the general area, as something akin to sacred ground, something to do with an ancient Druid grove and a great circle of stone rings, both of which had been uprooted and destroyed to make room for my new home, the great stones themselves smashed and used in the very foundations of the house itself. This and more he told me until I could contain myself no longer and laughed uproariously in the poor man's face. After some small while, I regained my composure and apologised profusely for my rudeness, all the while explaining that the local fairy tales bothered me not at all and the opinions of a bunch of superstitious locals bothered me even less. But still, I had to live in this place and do business with the shopkeepers and merchants, and so sent Wills on his way with a heavy purse with which to compensate the grieving families of the two men.

January 1837

Christmas was something of a muted affair. Many of my old friends and acquaintances are situated in London and we are quite alone here in our own little corner of the world. My wife does not partake of strong drink, as is becoming of a lady, and was somewhat silent and sullen through the whole affair. As for her maid, Matilda, she would not even acknowledge the sacred holiday at all and I fear she is no true Christian!

I stayed up late that night and drank deeply, lonely in my solitude. I even went so far as to drag my poor man servant, Stevens, from his warm bed before plying him liberally with generous amounts of finest Brandy. We sat there for some time before a roaring fire, talking over old times while the wind howled and gibbered outside our window. The last thing I heard as I fell asleep was the roar of the ocean. I did not dream.

March 1837

It has been four months and three days since we first moved into the house and, although I have taken my beautiful Elizabeth to bed every night and performed my husbandly duties with great vim and vigour, there is still no sign of a child. My beloved tells me these things take time but I find myself growing more sullen, spending more and more time locked in my study pouring over my old ledgers. My wife is strong, young and beautiful, and almost twenty years my junior. I fear our troubles stem from myself, for I have grown old in my many years of business, and now fear I shall never sire an heir to continue the sacred name of Vandraven. Oh God save me from such a fate!

April 1837

The doctor I sent for arrived only yesterday and, after a lengthy examination of both myself and Elizabeth, and following many searching questions, deemed us both fit and healthy and could see no reason why children should not be forthcoming in our immediate future.

September 1837

The summer was a glorious one and I had almost forgotten this journal. Our days have been spent frolicking on the local beaches where we picnicked and swam frequently in the chilly Cornish seas, our nights spent sipping wine on the veranda, listening to the gentle lapping of the surrounding sea but for all our happiness and our nightly devotions to one another, still, there is no sign of a child.

October 1837

God forgive me for I have sinned. I have drank of vile potions and have prayed to dark gods, offering up sacrifice for their favour. It all started with the witch, Matilda, who one evening, long after my wife had retired to her bed, approached me where I sat reading by lamp light in my study. She entered silently and I only noticed her presence when she laid a dusky hand upon my shoulder, causing me to cry out and spill my drink on the book I had been reading. Leaping to my feet, I cursed her roundly. She took a step back before my anger and curtsied, casting her eyes down demurely. Yet still, it seemed a small smile played across her shapely lips. I asked, no demanded, she explain why she was sneaking around the house at this ungodly hour instead of attending her mistress, my good lady wife. She informed me that her mistress was abed and sleeping soundly and it was now me she intended to serve! Baffled, I asked her meaning but her next question caught me off guard. She asked me how badly I wanted a child, and a male one at that, an heir to carry on the Vandraven bloodline. For a moment, I was tempted to beat her for her insolence and even raised my hand to do so but something in her eyes stilled my hand, causing it to drop limply by my side. Anything, I answered, I would do almost anything for a male heir to carry on the Vandraven name. Nodding, she took my hand and I marvelled at how soft her skin was against my own as she led me from my study through to the kitchen and down the darkened cellar below.

God how to describe what waited for me deep in the bowels of my own home! An altar! An altar anointed with blood, a sacrifice to some dark and terrible god. Everywhere candles burned, flickering in the eyes of the dead animals that lay all about. Pigeons, doves, cats and even a large black dog lay piled around its base, their blood soaking into the feet of that terrible statue that sat hunched and grotesque, an insult to those of us who dwell in the sane light of day. Its body, while hunched and twisted, resembled that of a man but that's where anything human in likeness suddenly stopped for its head was that of a great octopus scaled with huge staring eyes and a mass of withering tentacles covering the lower half of its face. From its gnarled back sprung stunted wings and its scaled arms and feet were claw like and webbed. I turned to run, to flee this abomination, but the witch Matilda stood blocking my way. I tried to push past but she grabbed my arm and span me back about to face her, blowing some kind of noxious dust in my face that instantly caused my head to pound and sent my senses reeling.

The next thing I knew we were both naked, kneeling before the bloody altar. The knife was in my hand. God, oh God, Stevens lay dead before me, his throat a red ruin, his hot blood all over me. Beside me knelt Matilda chanting, her naked body covered in sweat and blood as she cried out her devotion to her infernal gods. I tried to rise but she pushed me back down upon my back and climbed on top of me. From behind her, she pulled a small wooden bowl brimming with some noxious liquid, which she raised to her lips. Taking the potion into her mouth, she pressed her lips against my own but I twisted my head to and fro, raising my hands to beat her off but she caught them easily and placed them upon her heavy breast, letting some of the crimson potion trickle from between her ripe lips down over her heaving glistening body. I felt myself growing erect and knew I was lost as she enfolded me in her hot core, riding me back and forth until I cried out in ecstasy. In that moment, her lips crushed against mine, spilling the vile potion down my throat!

The rest of the night was filled with blurred images as we fornicated amongst the dead, like wild animals biting and tearing at each other, and I filled with all the vigour of youth, spilling my seed into her wanton flesh over and over again until at last I collapsed exhausted, only to awake the very next day battered and bruised in my own bed, so exhausted I was barely able to move. I called out and my cry was instantly heeded as a smiling Elizabeth entered the room carrying a tray as if she had been waiting just outside the door. She asked me how I was feeling as she placed the tray across my lap and told me how they had found me sweating and delirious upon my study floor in the grip of some strange fever. I tried to speak to tell her of the horror but I only managed a single word: Stevens. Smiling, she patted my hand, her next words turning my blood cold. "Sick," she lied, smiling all the while, "down with the same fever as your own, my love, but don't worry," she said, beginning to spoon feed me a strange tasting broth. "It will all be over soon."

November 1837

Days have passed, maybe even weeks. I am a prisoner laying here in this filthy bed, drugged and alone, only this journal to bear witness to my plight. The witch, Matilda, came to visit me yesterday, her belly already round and swollen. She took my hand and placed it on her stomach.

"What a fine son I will have," she grinned. "A fine boy who will have a fine name and a fine fortune, a vessel for my master, for now his time has come round once again, and he will walk abroad once more in the land of men and they will tremble at his coming, for the sleeper has awoken, Lucas Vandraven." She stroked my brow, almost affectionately, "and he will be of one father and two mothers, as it is written in the dark pages of time!" I could do nothing but lay there and listen to her ramblings as she spoon fed the intoxicating broth down my throat, her soft chanting lulling me into a drug fuelled sleep.

I awoke sometime later in the dark. Perhaps only hours had passed, or even days. It's so hard to keep track of time in this place. The last face I remembered seeing was that of my once beloved Elizabeth who sat silently by my side, spooning scalding broth between my lips, seeming to smile at whatever little pain she could cause me.

"How glad I will be when you are dead," she said, ramming the spoon down my throat until I started to gag and choke. "All those nights with your shrivelled old cock in me, sweating on me, grunting. How I shuddered at your touch, and still you couldn't give me a child. Now Matilda has the honour of bringing our master into the world but he is strong and will need two mothers and I will feel his sacred touch, feel him growing inside of me, and after, when he is born into this world, I will come for you, Lucas Vandraven." She raised and threw back the soiled covers from my wasted body. She poured the remainder of the scalding broth onto my naked lap and laughed down at me where I withered in agony before mercifully passing out.

Later, I felt a cold hand pressed against my throat as I swam up through the darkness.

"He is still alive," the voice of Matilda chimed. "You gave him too large a dose is all, that and the pain you have inflicted upon him."

"Why do we bother," Elizabeth replied. "Let's just kill him and have done with it."

"Be silent, you fool," Matilda snapped. "We still may have need of him. Should the ceremony go wrong, we will have to start the whole process all over again."

"Start again," Elizabeth's voice sounded worried. "As he is now, he can barely move, let alone give you another vessel for the master." Matilda laughed a throaty chuckle.

"I have potions that can rouse a dead man's passions, have no fear of that. If all goes well tomorrow night, we shall have no more use for him and you can kill him yourself but, until that time, leave him alone. No more of your little games."

"You promise," she asked, their voices moving away, "that I can kill him," fading now as they closed the door gently behind them. I knew then that I must find a way to stop them, not only for myself but also to prevent whatever evil they intended to bring into this world. God, I pray, give me strength!

This will be my last entry in this journal. I awoke this very night to the roar of thunder and the flash of lightening outside my window. It seemed I had slept the entire day away uninterrupted and felt somewhat better for it. Faded was the leaden feel in my limbs and my mind felt clear and sharp for the first time in many days. It seemed Elizabeth had heeded the witch Matilda's words and had left me alone or perhaps they were busy with whatever evil they were planning and had forgotten all about me. Either way, my prayers had been answered and I felt stronger than I had in days, now free from the effects of whatever terrible drug they had been feeding me!

Rousing myself, I sat up, wincing at the stiffness in my limbs as I slowly rose to my feet, leaning heavily against the bed post as a wave of dizziness assailed my senses. After some few deep breaths, the room stopped its spinning and I was able to gather my senses about me once again. Staggering over to my dresser, I quickly dressed before heading to the door. My hand had just started to turn the handle when the chanting started and suddenly the air felt charged with electricity, making it hard to breathe, causing my scalp to tighten and the skin of my arms to crawl with great knots of goose flesh.

For a moment, I considered running, leaving this place of the damned forever, but I could not. Whatever evil was afoot, I had played my part in it. For was it not my very essence that was being used, manipulated to bring something unspeakable into the world? Strengthening my resolve, I took a deep breath and threw open the door, expecting to be greeted by all the denizens of hell but there was only a darkened corridor lit by flashes of lightening and the crash of thunder that seemed to accompany that hellish chanting like some terrible drum. The air felt thick and heavy as I continued on down the hall, passed the library and drawing room till at last I stopped outside my wife's dressing room and, with trembling hands, threw open the door.

They were both there laying upon the floor, facing each other completely naked, their legs splayed wide open, their ankles entwined. The room was lit by hundreds of candles and there was blood everywhere. It lay in puddles upon the hardwood floor and ran in rivulets down the walls. Even the ceiling dripped with a crimson rain, splashing and hissing against the burning candles, splattering and showering the two chanting women. As I watched on in horror, Matilda's ripe stomach started to heave and twist. She had time to let out a single ear-piercing shriek before her stomach exploded, bathing Elizabeth's lower half in blood and gore as the creature inside her clawed and heaved its way out. I let out a wail of despair as the creature more fully emerged, for I had seen this thing before carved in stone deep in the bowels of my own home. For this was Matilda's dark god brought to life by our terrible union.

At the sound of my cry, Elizabeth, noticing my presence for the first time, raised her blood covered face and hissed at me. Her eyes filled with hatred as if daring me to come closer. Now the creature was free and slowly crawling towards her waiting flesh, a leprous umbilical cord trailing behind it, eager to be in its new host hidden away from the world where it could continue to grow and consolidate its power. Quickly, I looked for something, anything I could use as a weapon. My eyes fell upon a basket full of knitting. With a cry of triumph, I leaped forward and snatched up two slender wooden needles and ran across the room but it was too late. The creature was gone, hidden away, buried deep inside my once beloved Elizabeth. Only the trailing umbilical cord remained.

Stealing myself, I made a grab for it, snatching it up. At once, my skin began to burn and blister where the thing twisted and writhed in my hand. With a cry of fear and outrage, I heaved with all my might, aborting the hateful thing back into the world. I did not stop or even think but thrust the wooden needles down, driving them deep through the creature's strange flesh, pinning it in place. It let out a scream, a screech that only the truly damned could ever muster, shrivelling my poor shrunken soul, reverberating through the halls of my mind, then it lay still, the glow fading from its glaring yellow eyes once again, cheated, banished back to whatever strange hell it had come from!

Elizabeth was climbing to her feet.

"The master," she cried. "Oh Lucas, what have you done to our son?" But I let her say no more. Grabbing her by the hair, I reached down and yanked the needles from the now dead abomination and thrust them upwards under her chin into the soft flesh of her throat. Her eyes widened and she staggered away, gurgling and tugging at them, widening the wound till blood pored like a river down her body, mixing with the already blood soaked floor, causing her to slip and fall, sending her crashing into a nearby dressmaker's dummy which she clung to, trying to find her balance. But it was too late. Her legs gave way and she dragged the thing down on top of her, pinning her beneath, as she convulsed and writhed, reaching out towards me, her fingers clutching, pleading, begging but I turned my face from her. When I looked back, it was finally over.

And so it has ended and only I remain. I have written all through the long night and at last the sun rises, driving back the darkness, but it can never drive away the darkness within or the stain upon my soul. I shall go to the cliff's edge now. I shall take my only son and heir with me. Together we shall travel through dark waters. May God have mercy on our souls!

CLOTTED CREAM

He stood on the wet cobble stones of the outer harbour and looked out over the still waters of Mevagissey Bay. To his right stood the Mevagissey lighthouse, all rust and peeling paint. He patted it fondly as he passed, heading back towards the inner harbour and the centre of the village. He liked to stand and look out over the harbour. He supposed it had become something of a ritual whenever he came here. His was a tiresome job and he found small pleasures whenever he could. Not that he ever had that much time. Not only was his job tiresome, it was time consuming as well.

Talking of time, he looked up at where the sun appeared between the lazy summer clouds and saw that it was nearly noon. Picking up his pace, he strolled past the Mevagissey Aquarium where sunkissed parents laughed as chocolate covered children looked in awe at the bounty of the surrounding seas. He didn't linger but moved on passed bustling shops where the summer people sifted through varnished shells and fishing memorabilia from days of old. Nobody noticed the backpack, casually tossed under one of the many tourist filled benches. It was faded denim, covered in badges and peeling stickers. He supposed people believed that it could well belong to one of the many people by their side, enjoying a lunchtime pasty or a vinegar soaked portion of fish and chips. Either way, in this day and age, people should be more wary of such things. He shrugged and moved on. Such things were none of his concern. He had a job to do. How it got done was none of his business. Only the end result mattered.

Time was growing short now. He could feel it in his bones. Nevertheless, he couldn't help but stop at an ice-cream parlour, a little emptier than the rest, and admire the many flavours and colours that lay behind the glass like ice shrouded flowers. Reluctantly, he turned away and found an empty seat, a rarity in itself this time of year, and looked out at the boats that rocked to and fro on the still waters of the harbour.

The explosion came seconds later in a roaring fury of fire, metal, stone and blood. In the aftermath, survivors screamed and bled, children wept, fathers groaned and mothers screamed their children's names. He stood, untouched and unfazed by the devastation about him. Turning, he straightened his robes and picked up his scythe. Winter was usually his busiest time in such a small, quiet place but he had a feeling this summer was going to be a real bitch.

THE DRESSMAKER'S DUMMY

Eric Michaels didn't like the dressmaker's dummy as soon as he laid eyes on it. Then again, he was already prepared to hate anything his wife, Sarah, brought back from the Vandraven House. If ever there was a haunted house, a truly haunted house, the Vandraven House was it. The site of both multiple murder and suicide, it sat overlooking the village like some broken idol for nearly three hundred years. The place was cursed, damned, and Eric Michaels wanted nothing to do with it and he sure as hell didn't want anything from that decrepit wreck in his home. But when Sarah had heard there was to be an auction there, she had promptly lost her mind and immediately called up her friend, Marsha, arranging to meet at the Vandraven estate promptly at eight the following morning.

Eric could well imagine them both sat outside the front gate like a couple of vultures decked out in their best summer dresses, just waiting for the poor auctioneer to open the doors so they could sweep in and pick over the fallen carcass of the Vandraven House. In the end, she had returned with only two purchases: a dressmaker's dummy and a dusty set of crystal cut wine glasses that Eric told her he would never drink from. She had laughed at him then, calling him a superstitious fool before patting him fondly on the cheek and returning to the meticulous cleaning of her new found treasures.

Eric sighed and left her to it. It was all very well for her to call him a fool but she was an out of towner from 'up country' as the locals were fond of saying. Eric had been born and bred in Mevagissey. He had heard the stories passed on from generation to generation, had gathered in tents on many a Halloween night and listened with terrified fascination as his friends, and sometimes their older brothers, told gruesome stories of Lucas Vandraven who had slaughtered his wife, unborn child and even his few servants before throwing himself from a nearby cliff, stories of the Jonas family found dead in the basement of that house, their bodies twisted as if by some terrible force. She had never scurried passed the house as a child, walking home alone from school as the sunset made the cracked and shattered windows burn with a seemingly evil intent.

Yes, the Vandraven House was as much a part of the village as the fishing boats in the harbour and the summer people who came to visit every year. One day, he supposed, when the old place became decrepit enough, they would pull it down and then all the evil things inside would rest. But for now, it still stood, a monument to madness, a madness that had now spread to his home.

The first real argument started when Sarah moved the dressmaker's dummy into their bedroom. Eric had seen the Godawful thing stood in the corner of the large bay window next to Sarah's sewing machine and had promptly flipped out. There was no way he was getting even one minute's sleep with that ugly looking thing looming over him. But Sarah was having none of it. The whole thing devolved into a shouting match, where Eric threatened to sleep on the sofa till the damn thing was gone with Sarah storming out, telling him he was welcome to it.

She had left him sat there on the bed fuming, wanting to scoop the fucking thing up and throw it down the stairs after her but not quite daring to do so. Instead, he stood up and slowly crossed the room, wondering what the hell she saw in something so ugly.

The dummy was typical of its kind: legless, armless, it was nothing more than a headless torso impaled on a tarnished brass stand. The material covering the body looked to Eric like a light hessian, torn and ripped in many places. The overall feel of the thing was one of age and neglect. Curious now, he slid off the bed down to his knees and peered underneath, looking for a date or even a maker's mark. What he saw there caused him to recoil in horror.

The underside of the thing was covered in a dark maroon stain that could only be blood, old and dry, but blood nevertheless. The bottom was covered in it, drenched in it. Reaching out with a trembling hand, he touched the stains and was suddenly falling, the room spinning, disappearing as if he were being pulled down some black tunnel.

The room was gone, replaced by something else, somewhere else. All about him burnt candles, hundreds of candles and blood. There was blood everywhere. It lay in puddles upon the hardwood floor, ran in rivulets down the walls. Even the ceiling dripped with a crimson rain, splashing and hissing where it made contact with the flickering candles, filling the air with its choking scent.

Reaching down with a hand that was no longer his own, he pulled two wooden knitting needles from the abomination that lay dead at his feet and span around. A woman was climbing to her feet quite naked and covered in blood. "The master!" she sobbed. "Oh Lucas, what have you done to our son?" Again that terrible hand reached out, grabbing the woman by the hair and thrusting the needles into the soft flesh of her throat. She staggered away, gurgling blood gushing from her mouth as she tugged at the needle buried deep in her throat. Slipping, she cried out, grabbing at a nearby dressmaker's dummy, clinging on for dear life, pulling at it, raking it with her nails as she pulled it down on top of her, pinning her beneath. She reached out begging, pleading, but he was going away now back into the blackness, back to before, to now, to here, to this place.

With a cry, he opened his eyes and yelled out in disgust. He was holding the dressmaker's dummy, holding it tight to his chest like some terrible dance partner. Thrusting it away, he backed up, trying to look everywhere at once. Dizzy, disorientated, he tripped over the corner of the bedroom rug, crashing to the floor, his head hitting the radiator with terrible force. The pain was blinding, turning his vision red then mercifully he passed out into blackness.

He awoke two days later with fourteen stitches and a bad concussion. Sarah had found him unconscious on the bedroom floor, his head lying in a pool of his own blood and had immediately called for an ambulance. He had only awoken once in the back of the ambulance as it rushed him towards St Austell General but his words had been slurred and nonsensical, something about candles and blood, before he passed out again. But now, he was awake and doing well. His doctor had told him he would be able to go home at the end of the week, after a few more days of observation.

For the next few days, he lay there, the tedium only broken by meal times and Sarah's frequent visits. At night time, he would lay awake, staring at the ceiling, wondering what he was going to do about the dressmaker's dummy. There was no way he could tell Sarah what had happened. She would think he had hit his head a little too hard. Besides, she would never believe him, and who could blame her. He barely believed it himself. He knew only one thing: the damn thing had to go but how to get rid of it? That was the question.

He was still pondering that same question on the night they released him from hospital. It was seven thirty that night and Eric was standing outside the hospital entrance, doing his best not to obstruct the automatic sliding doors that kept opening and closing, much to the annoyance of the on-call duty nurse at reception, as he tried to take shelter from the pouring rain.

Sarah should have been here to pick him up over half an hour ago but she hadn't shown up. Worried, Michael rang the house but the phone was engaged. He tried two more times with the same results before trying her mobile, which rang for a couple of minutes then cut to her answering machine. Eric had a sudden sense of foreboding so strong that he actually became light headed and nearly dropped his mobile phone as he leaned heavily against the side of the building.

After a few deep breaths, he quickly dialled the number of their good friend and neighbour, Helen Daniels. Thankfully, she answered on the second ring and was more than happy to go knock on the door and see what Sarah was up to. No, Michael didn't mind waiting. Michael stood there sweating and listening to the silence for what seemed like forever but in less than five minutes, Helen was back telling him, yes, the car was still there and no, no one was answering the door and yes, it was locked and all the lights were on.

Eric hung up on Helen before she could start asking questions and called for a taxi. Less than ten minutes later, he was speeding towards home.

Stepping out into the rain soaked street, he paid the taxi driver and turned to face the house. Just like Helen had said, the car was still in the drive and the house was lit up like a Christmas tree, with both the upstairs and downstairs lights switched on. Feeling a little more relieved, Eric tried the front door and, finding it locked just like Helen had said, he dug in his pocket and pulled out his keys. Stepping into the porch, he opened the door into the hall and suddenly stopped, his wife's name dying on his lips.

The hall phone was hanging by its cord, gently swinging back and forth. Sarah's handbag was lying on the floor, its contents scattered and strewn all about and the stairs, Jesus God the stairs, were covered in blood. It was splattered all over the banister, slowly running down the wall in rivulets, soaking into the carpet beneath. Hitching, hardly able to breathe, Michael staggered back into the porch and vomited nosily into the corner. He stayed that way, holding onto the wall, sweating and shivering, until his stomach stopped its twitching and, heaving for a moment, he considered just leaving. No one could lose that much blood and survive. But if there was a chance, even a small one...

He tried not to think as he ascended the stairs, feeling the blood squelching under his feet. On the landing was one of Sarah's shoes. It lay on its side and was filled with blood. Eric's nerve broke then and he turned to run, grabbing onto the sticky bannister to stop him falling headlong down the stairs. He was only halfway down when he suddenly stopped, reeling backwards. There was a woman at the bottom of the stairs. She was naked and covered in blood, a gaping hole in her throat. Michael screamed as he recognised the woman from his terrible vision. He tried to move, to run away, but he was frozen, unable to move.

The woman started up the stairs, her eyes glittering like black jewels. Michael looked on in horror as she smiled up at him, revealing rotting teeth from which dark blood began to ooze. Letting out a cry of terror, his paralysis broke and he turned, fleeing up the stairs, passed the bedroom door, meaning to lock himself in the bathroom but suddenly she appeared right in front of his face.

"Our son," she screamed, splattering his face with her noxious blood. Terrified, half blinded, he scrambled backwards, trying to wipe her vileness from his face. Screaming, she lunged forward, shoving him hard in the chest, sending him crashing through the bedroom door and onto the floor. His already battered head glanced off the bedroom table and, for a moment, the world darkened and he feared he would pass out.

Groaning, he raised himself up onto his elbows, trying to look everywhere at once but the doorway was empty. Sobbing with relief, he clambered to his feet, ignoring the throbbing in his head. Suddenly, he was sure she was behind him, ready to wrap her cold dead hands around his throat and, with a cry, he span around, his hands held high in a warding off gesture. But the woman was not there, only his wife Sarah. For a moment, Eric Michaels was not sure what he was seeing then he began to laugh. The laughter turned into a scream, the scream a shriek as he clawed at his face, at his eyes, desperate not to see yet unable to look away.

The dressmaker's dummy stood in its usual place but now a bloody crumpled figure lay at its base. Bone and sinew gleamed wetly under the merciless glare of the overhead light. The torn and battered body would have been unrecognisable except for Sarah's head where it now sat atop the shoulders of the dressmaker's dummy, her eyes rolled back to white, her blood covered mouth wrenched open in a silent scream. The blood from the ragged stump of her neck ran down onto what was left of her tattered skin, which had been stitched and sewn with crude stitches onto the dressmaker's dummy.

As he looked on with horror, the whole thing began to vibrate, the empty arms starting to twist and turn, reaching out towards him. Still screaming, he started to back away. He heard laughter, then, not with his ears but echoing round the broken vaults of his mind and suddenly realised Sarah's poor dead lips were writhing, showing her bloody teeth. Her eyes now watched him, glaring at him as the vibrations grew stronger, getting closer and closer.

The police found him there a few hours later, after an anonymous call, raving and ranting, his mind broken as he cradled the head of his poor murdered wife in his arms.

As for the dressmaker's dummy, there was no sign.

In the Vandraven House, time did not stand still. It crawled and undulated. In the library, ancient books tumbled from wooden shelves. In the hall, the sound of booted heels scrabbled on the winding staircase. In the kitchen, an ear-piercing scream was followed by breaking glass, then stillness. In this silence, a grandfather clock ticked and the house waited, and waited, and waited.

THE WELL

Jonah Matheson rose with the rising sun, ate a bowl of porridge, gathered up his tools and headed out towards the fields. He was just passing through the centre of the village when a figure emerged out of the early dawn mist.

Jonah drew up short. Shocked by the man's sudden appearance, he gave a startled cry, sending his tools clattering to the ground. With a curse, he snatched up his shovel and headed over to the figure standing silently by the old town well.

As he approached, the stranger turned more fully towards him, showing somewhat more of his profile. The man was tall, his hair swept back from a high clear brow. He wore a long dark trench coat and in his hand he carried a battered looking valise. The white collar of a priest adorned his neck.

Jonah had intended to question the man. As village headsman, he knew the shape and form of every man, woman and child that lived in Homestead village. Long experience also told him that none of them would be up and about at this ungodly hour of the morning, except perhaps for old Tom Davis, the village baker, but he wouldn't be wasting his time lurking around some old disused well. Tom would be stoking up his ovens, ready for the morning's bake.

As he drew closer, he felt the first worm of fear thread its way through his guts and tried to push it away but with little success. Jonah did not like priests. As a boy, he had been terrified by sermons of hellfire and brimstone delivered by the wild eyed Father Gilychrist in what was now the ruined St Antony's. Then, there had been stories of missing children, a fire and the mystery of the missing priest.

The man turned more fully now at Jonah's approach and, smiling, extended his hand.

"Father Thomas," he said, by way of introduction.

"Jonah Matherson." His hand was swallowed in a grip that felt immensely powerful and was pumped a single time then dropped. Jonah resisted the urge to wipe his hand on his jean-clad leg. There was something about the man's touch he didn't like. His skin felt rough and dry, like shaking hands with a snake. The man had already turned back to his contemplation of the well.

"Your well has run dry," he said, running a large hand over the rough block work, watching as the loose mortar crumbled under his touch. "I was thirsty after my long journey but there seems to be some kind of blockage at the bottom. The whole thing is in disrepair." Jonah, sensing some kind of accusation, answered brusquely.

"Yes, it is blocked and it will stay that way."

"I see," the priest said, turning to consider the blackened ruins of the old church that lay in the neighbouring meadow, half turning to face Jonah as if reluctant to take his eyes from the burnt out shell of St Antony's. "You know there are rumours about this place in and around the local area, talk of heathen practices, sacrifices, and maybe even talk of this very well being used in some kind of terrible ritual." Hearing this, Jonah moved up close to the other man and spun him about to face him. If the taller man was intimated, he did not show it.

"This is the year of our Lord, Eighteen Eighty Seven. It is not the dark ages and such heathen ways are not practised in Homestead."

"Not any more," the other man countered with a sly smile.

"Who are you?" Jonah demanded. "What do you know of us?"

"I told you who I am. I am Father Thomas Gilychrist, sent here by Mother Church to put an end to your heathen ways."

Jonah, taken aback by the mention of the man's name stammered, "there are no heathens here! Not since my father became headman, and myself after him. You will find only good Christians in this village."

"Glad to hear it," the priest said, turning and walking away in the direction of the blackened church.

"You said your name was Gilychrist," Jonah called after him, but there was no reply, only a darkening shadow as the man vanished into the whirling mist.

Jonah abandoned all thoughts of farming and turned from the fields, heading back for home. His mind was swirling with half formed accusations. How much did this stranger know and was he even a stranger? That name, that Godforsaken name, Gilychrist. The old woman would know. She was old as Methuselah, her teeth all gone, balding and scabrous. Still, he loved the old woman, his grandmother, who had put ointment on his cut knees as a child and showed him where fairy rings grew in the forest. Yes, he thought, taking the stairs two at a time, the old woman would know what to do.

He knocked on the door, knowing that she would be awake. She rarely slept more than a couple of hours these days. She was sat upright in her bed as he entered, her gnarled hands folded primly in her lap, almost as if she had been expecting him.

"You have news," she said, peering at him closely through cloudy eyes as he paced the room. He stopped, turning to her.

"News, yes, something to tell you," he said, taking a seat beside her. "But I am not sure where to start."

"Tell me anyway," she said, reaching for his hand. "A burden shared is a burden halved." He took the offered hand gently in his own and thought for a moment, trying to gather his wits and wondering where to begin.

"Tell me of Richard Gilychrist, the priest who ruled St Antony's before the big fire." The old woman jumped as if stung and pulled her hand free.

"Why do you want to know of such things!" He drew back from the old woman's venom, startled by her outburst. "What has happened? Tell me," she demanded.

"Alright, alright. There was a stranger in the village this morning, standing by the old well. He claimed to be a priest and said his name was

Gilychrist." The old woman drew in a sharp breath, clutching at her chest. She scrambled for the glass of water at her bedside table. Jonah was by her side instantly. Drawing the old woman close, he put the glass of water into her shaking hands and held her until the spasms that racked her frail body started to pass.

"It's alright. I am alright, now. Go sit down, boy. Give me space to breathe. It was the shock, that's all. I haven't heard that name in nearly forty years. Tell me everything, everything he said to you, what he looked like, everything." Jonah did as he was bid. By the time he had finished, his grandmother looked smaller, frailer somehow. "Tell me about the well," she said. "One more time, word for word. What did he say about the well?"

"He said our well had run dry, that it was in disrepair, and asked how long it had been that way. When I answered him, he told me that there were rumours about the village, as if we didn't already know. Talk of heathen practices. I felt like he was laughing at me, laughing at us!" The old woman contemplated this for a time.

"You asked me to tell you of Richard Gilychrist and I will, though it is something we have never spoken of. First, I must know what you know of him and that old well. Tell me these things then I will tell you the truth, so help me God."

"I remember my old friend, Timmy Charles," Jonah said, quietly. "We used to play out in the yard, our bare bottoms in the dirt. That was until the well ran dry. I remember him being put into the bucket. The whole town was there, all except Timmy's mother and father. The priest, he was there, standing side by side with my Grandaddy, your husband, and my father. It was my father that put Timmy in the bucket and placed something on his head."

"Hawthorne," the old woman interrupted softy. "It was a crown of Hawthorne."

"My father told Timmy that the well was blocked and that he must unblock it so that the crops would grow again, and the people of the village would be happy. Then they lowered him down. I remember my father had tears running down his face and all the while my Grandaddy and that accursed priest were chanting and reading from some great book. A book that looked like no bible that I had ever seen and that was the end of it. When the bucket was raised, Timmy was gone. I remember people just walking away like they didn't even care that Timmy had gotten lost in the well. I ran over screaming, calling Timmy's name over and over again. My father gently pulled me away, picking me up and crooning softly in my ear, telling me it was for the best, that it had to be done so the village could live. Shortly after that, Grandaddy died and the church was destroyed in the fire. After, as I grew up, I seemed to hear stories everywhere I went, of how Homestead village was a cursed place. Even as a young man, trading at the annual farmers' markets, men were hard pressed to buy and sell to Homestead folks. Is that it, old mother? Are we cursed?" The old woman sighed.

"We cursed ourselves," she whispered, "but we had help from that devil, Gilychrist. It all started with the building of St Antony's. We lost our old church, St Hilda's, in the great storm of Eighteen Thirty. I was still young back then and your father was just reaching his manhood. It was a foul night when the wind blew off the sea like all the devils of hell were abroad that night. People slept in their cellars and many a thatched roof was ruined, destroyed, even blown completely away in the great gales. But it was the old church that suffered the most.

Come morning, there was nothing but shattered stone and rotten timbers left and poor Father Roberts crushed to death inside. It was your grandfather, ever a pious man, who wrote to the diocese in Truro, informing the bishop of the calamity that had struck the village and requesting funds to build a new place of worship. Most important of all, he asked for a new priest to replace poor old Father Roberts.

Within a month, a man arrived on horseback, carrying a hefty bag of coins and a letter from the bishop giving us express permission to build a new church on the site of the doomed St Hilda's. The man was tall, dark and handsome as the devil. He introduced himself as Father Richard Gilychrist and told us he was here to oversee the construction of our new church and to see to our spiritual well-being. So we had our funding and our new priest.

Your grandfather, with your father by his side, hired an architect, workmen, builders and carpenters from the surrounding area and got straight to work, digging a strong foundation for our new church. That is where the trouble started. After the rubble of the old church was cleared away, the architect, Mr Landsford from Truro who had built churches in Gorran, Mevagissey and St David's, took one look at the old church foundations and shook his head. He told us of his amazement that our old church had stood for so long, the foundations being so shallow and poorly sunken. So the men of the village started work, digging out new foundations and it was at this time that they found the old ruins that would bring so much heartache to so many.

At first, the work was easy going but as the men dug down deeper, they started hitting hard rock and stone. It was your grandfather that found the entrance to the catacombs beneath. He told me later how he had cleared away dirt and gravel from a large flat stone that held some kind of strange engravings. With the help of the other men, and after much sweating and cursing, they had managed to push the great stone aside, revealing stone steps leading down into the darkness. Your grandfather had sent for oil lamps and, at once, with your father and the new priest, Gilychrist, by his side, had started down into the darkness.

At first, the walls had been rough, nitre streaked and covered with chisel marks, but as they slowly descended, the walls had smoothed out. The lights from their flickering lamps had revealed hieroglyphs of such an obscene nature that your grandfather was hard pressed to describe their likeness! He mentioned strange shambling figures, dragging women and small children towards a great lake where abhorrent creatures lay waiting by the shore side, their claw tipped hands reaching out for screaming victims.

As they descended further down the narrow, dripping tunnel, they began to hear the sound of rushing water. They traversed a sharp bend in the tunnel then came to a sudden halt, their mouths hanging askew. The tunnel had opened up into a huge cavern where rushing water fed into a great lake before disappearing back underground. The entire scene was dimly lit by a small hole in the crumbling ceiling and, as the men watched, a bucket came splashing down into the great lake and slopping water was slowly pulled upwards. The sound of women's laughter suddenly echoed around the cavern's vastness and all three men understood that this was the river-fed lake that supplied Homestead's well with its water.

Your father, seeing the great lake, and unnerved by the obscene hieroglyphs above, demanded that they return to the surface at once. Gilychrist, however, had let out a shout of excitement and before either man could restrain him had gone running and stumbling down the last few stone steps onto the cavern floor. That's when your grandfather saw the ancient ruin, a stone temple, which was carved into the very rock face itself and situated down by the gently lapping shores of the lake.

Grabbing your father by his shirt sleeve, they ran after the frantic priest, their lanterns throwing strange shadows all about them. They arrived just in time to see Gilychrist slip between two leaning pillars as he headed inside the crumbling ruin. Moments later, there was a ghastly scream. Most men would have fled at such a cry of terror, echoing in such a terrible place, but the two men were made of sterner stuff and quickly followed inside. What they saw was like a scene from a nightmare!

In one corner, Gilychrist sat rocking back and forth with some great leather bound book gripped tight in his nerveless fingers. Looming above him was a great statue that rose high into the darkness above, a large black, stained altar before it. Never had the men seen its like before. Its aspect was that of a great worm, a leech, a parasitic thing that seemed to belong in the outer realms of madness. It seemed to lean towards them with a blind unspeakable hunger.

Gilychrist whimpered, "the floor, God save us, look at the floor!" The two men dragged their eyes away from the looming monstrosity above them and, lowering their lanterns, they gazed in horror at the temple floor.

The floor was littered with shattered bones, gaping skulls and tatters of mouldering cloth. With a cry your father turned, crushing the skull of a small child underfoot as he fled. Your grandfather dragged the sobbing priest to his feet and started to run, pushing the other man forward as they fled from that place of terror and madness into the cleansing light above. Gasping for breath, covered in dirt and grime, they burst out from the tunnels below with Gilychrist still clutching that great tome to his chest. The workers immediately surrounded them, bombarding them with questions, asking them what had happened, demanding to know what they had seen below. In the chaos that ensued, Richard Gilychrist slipped away."

Jonah shook himself as if coming out of a trance. His grandmother had always been a good story teller but this was one such story he wished he had not heard and yet he knew with a heavy heart there was still more to come.

"What happened next?" he asked in a whisper. "What was in that Godforsaken book?" His grandmother, reached for her water glass and drank deeply.

"Yes, Godforsaken it was, written in bastard Latin. Your grandfather wouldn't let it rest, though. After three days when he barely ate a thing and slept like a stone, he went off to confront the priest. When he reached the dig site, however, he found the tunnels all filled in and covered with mortar. In the three days he had slept, Father Gilychrist had taken over the operation and hurriedly laid the foundations for the new St Antony's. Your grandfather took the smiling priest by the sleeve and pulled him to one side.

"Are you mad," he asked the other man. "You can't build a church here, not after what we saw down there. That place was evil, far and from the eyes of God!"

"No place is unseen by God, my son," Gilychrist continued smiling. "Besides, as you can see, every trace of the entrance is gone, sealed up, buried forever. Only yesterday, I blessed this very ground, consecrating it in Christ's name."

"Every trace?" your grandfather asked. "And what of that great book you brought up from that hell? What has become of it"

"It is in my care," Gilychrist replied, no longer smiling. "It is written in Latin, an ancient language that I have the honour of understanding."

"I wish to see it."

"Why?" Gilychrist asked, one eyebrow raised. "Do you read Latin?"

"You know I do not," your grandfather replied.

"Then I suggest you get back to work as there is still much to do," Gilychrist said, walking away.

"When your grandfather told me this, it was hard for me to believe. I liked Richard Gilychrist. He was tall, handsome but, above all, he was gentle. All that changed in the following months. In fact, many things changed in those dark months, including your grandfather. Firstly, there was the strange chanting. It came floating across the meadow from the direction of St Antony's.

The church was small and in the past month had come on in leaps and bounds. Father Gilychrist had been living in the rooms above the local tavern but once the slate roof had been added to the church and small rectory, he had moved straight in. It was upon that first night that the chanting was heard. Dogs howled in the night and people came to their doors to listen but then quickly disappeared back inside.

The following morning was Sunday and Father Richard held the first mass in his new church. The walls were cold stone and not yet plastered, and the wind blew through arched windows that held no glass. There were still no pews and the congregation had to kneel on the stone cold floor and that's where they stayed for the next three hours as Father Gilychrist preached the word of the Lord in ringing tones. He spoke of the Good Shepherd, of Cain and Able making sacrifice unto God, and of Abraham's test of faith when asked to sacrifice his son, Isaac. Finishing with a prayer asking God to bless and keep them safe, he bid them go in peace. As they arose from bloodied knees, Father Gilychrist smiled and quickly hurried away.

No-one asked questions about the strange chanting in the night.

It was as if Mother Earth herself had turned her face from us. Crops died without reason. There was no disease or ravenous plague of insects, they just died. Great fields of corn suddenly turned black and potatoes, almost ready for the harvest, turned to white mush in the ground. Every vegetable, fruit and grain in every field and garden, were all destroyed within the week. Fishermen's nets and crab pots came up empty. Homestead village was facing ruin. Not only were we going hungry but, without the revenue brought in from the farmer's market, we would have no money to buy the seeds needed to plant next year's harvest.

Still, the strange chanting in the night continued, and it was your grandfather who plucked up the courage to go out one night across the dark road and into the shadow of St Antony's. He didn't return until the wee small hours of the morning and from that night onwards he was never the same, becoming both cruel and harsh. He started spending his nights over at St Antony's, often returning stinking of liquor and mumbling strange words, his hair often in disarray and his eyes wild and tormented.

One night, I clung to his leg and begged him not to go, but he beat me with his belt until I passed out. When I awoke, I was in St Antony's bent over the altar with my hands tied. Father Gilychrist was thrusting himself in and out of me as your grandfather stood nearby. He was naked and holding a great book in his hand, chanting in some strange language that made my skin crawl. When Gilychrist was finished, my own husband raped me while the priest danced and laughed in the flickering candle light. At last, after I had been defiled in every way possible, they let me go.

I fled into the forest and stayed there for three days until your father came and found me. By then, more and more of the villagers had joined with Gilychrist and your grandfather. Virgins and widow women alike were defiled on the altar of St Antony's. When Gilychrist felt he had enough of the village in his power, he started talking about sacrifices and how God had abandoned us. Was it not God who had killed our crops and denied us the bounty of the sea, treating us no better than the plague tormented children of Egypt? But there were other gods, gods who were older and more powerful than the man God, Jesus. Gods that he could summon. He had found the way to restore the land in his book of power. Even your father was convinced for a little while, for never did a man love his father more than your father loved your grandfather. In his eyes, the man could do no wrong and, besides the great seducer, Gilychrist was as convincing as the devil that he had become.

Perhaps I am making excuses for them, but you must remember that the village was in ruin. Its people were half starved animals and even small babes were dying through lack of food. I am here to tell you that those people who did such terrible things were not evil, desperate yes, but not evil. Even Gilychrist had been a good man before whatever evil resided in that book had warped his mind and soul.

Five children went into that well, one every year, and always at harvest time. None ever returned and suddenly the village started to prosper once more. Crops started to push their way through the dark loamy soil, and fishing nets were almost filled to bursting. Animals fell pregnant and the woods and surrounding forest ran wild with game. The midnight orgies went on and on with Gilychrist residing over it all like some half crazed devil.

Your little friend, Timmy, was the last sacrifice. Up until that moment, your father had only been a bystander, not actively participating in any of the obscene rituals, though he had done nothing to stop your grandfather and Gilychrist. When it was time for young Timmy to be sent into the well, Gilychrist insisted it was your father's turn to make the sacrifice. He protested, of course, but was told by Gilychrist in no uncertain terms that you would take Timmy's place if he didn't do as he was bid. His young wife, your mother, would be taken up to the church that very night and forced to take part in the night's obscene rituals. Your father did as he was told and then walked away and went straight home.

I was there visiting with your mother when he came back. He walked in through the door with his head down and he spoke to no-one, but marched through the house, wrenched open the back door and vanished into the yard. He stayed out there all day, sharpening his axe and muttering darkly to himself. Even your mother, who your father loved dearly, didn't dare to go near him. At last, as the sun sank below the horizon and the night came on, the strange chanting and the screams of the violated began to fill the night air once more. Your father rose up, his axe over his shoulder gleaming dangerously in the moonlight, and again, without a word of farewell, lit a torch from the fire and left the house, heading out into the night.

What happened next I only found out some years later, as your father lay dying from the fever that killed him. By then, your poor mother was already five year dead, her and your poor unborn sister both. I was nursing your father, trying to break his fever when he started to moan and talk in his delirium. He grabbed my arm and began to speak.

"Killed him," he said, his eyes rolling in his head like a frightened mare, "my father your husband." I put my fingers to his lips but he twisted his head away. "Had to. He was in league with the devil, him and Gilychrist both! I locked them in the church," he said, grasping my arm tighter. "Barred the door while they were drinking and fucking. I saw them through the window. There was blood," he gasped. "Dead animals everywhere, their throats cut. Some of the people were drinking their blood, pouring it on themselves, rubbing it onto their bodies while others licked it off. Gilychrist sat naked on the altar, laughing and, Jesus, God, my father right in the middle of it all, rutting like some great beast!"

I tried to drag my arm away and begged him to be silent but he held me fast, the sweat running down his face as he relived that terrible night. "Yes, barred the door, stuck my axe through both handles. There was oil nearby, left over from the renovations of the church so I smashed a window, poured in the oil and threw in my torch. They didn't even notice until the flames licked at the walls. They stampeded for the door and, finding it locked, trampled over each other trying to climb through the narrow windows. Some had already started to burn as they tried to twist through but I had my sickle and hatchet stuck in my belt. It was a blood bath. I waded in, cutting them to pieces, sending their damn souls to hell. Finally, it was his turn for, as he came squirming through the window blackened and burned, I still recognised my own father. He fell heavily to the floor, the damp grass putting out the last of the flames and started to crawl towards me. His burnt and blackened hand grasped my boot and he tried to speak, but I brought the hatchet down on his head and ended his suffering. I waited all night. I sat there until the flames subsided and then I entered the church. There were bodies everywhere. I searched for Gilychrist but it was almost impossible to find his body amongst the burnt, blackened and twisted dead. I only hoped he had perished in the fire along with his crazed congregation. Forgive me, forgive my sins," he had said, laying back, his eyes fluttering closed, and his hand dropped away. Whether he was talking to me or God I do not know, for he never regained consciousness and died shortly after."

Jonah came to her then and tried to wipe away her tears, but she waved him away impatiently.

"Now this man has arrived in the village. Another Gilychrist. Yes, a strange coincidence, I would have said, before he mentioned the well. You described him as a young man, yet when Richard Gilychrist arrived in the village he must have been thirty years old at least. That was forty years ago, so you see it can't be the same man, Jonah. He would be seventy years old and an old man. Yet he has that cursed name and knows things about us that no outsider should know."

"What do you want me to do, Grandmother?" Jonah said, kneeling by her bedside. "Tell me what to do and it shall be done."

"Nothing. Go about your business as normal, work the fields and stay away from that accursed church. Tomorrow, when I am feeling stronger, I shall take a look at this Gilychrist and then we shall do whatever needs doing."

All day, Jonah worked the fields. He tried not to think, to let the familiar rhythm of work soothe his mind and ease his nerves, but the sound of his grandmother's voice and the horror of her terrible story, kept invading his mind. He worked faster and faster until, just as the sun started to set, he stumbled home. After quickly checking on his grandmother, who seemed to be sleeping soundly, he stripped off his sodden clothes and climbed into bed, falling into an exhausted sleep.

He awoke in the darkness and climbed out of bed. He tried to stop, to open his mouth, to scream. He had no control over his own body and was trapped, a screaming prisoner in his own head. His body moved outside into the night seemingly of its own volition. It was then that he heard the low chanting and saw the flickering torches surrounding the village well.

As he drew closer, other figures emerged from the darkness, his friends and neighbours. Their faces slack, their eyes vacant, and he knew that, like himself, they were trapped inside, unable to move, unable to resist. Others moved amongst them, robed and cowled figures holding flaming torches aloft. It was from these strange figures that the guttural chanting issued forth. Standing amongst them proud and tall, his face flickering in the torch light, stood the priest, Thomas Gilychrist. As the last of the villagers joined the circle, the robed figures stopped their chanting and silence descended. The priest took up a torch from one of the robed figures and started examining the trapped villagers. When he found Jonah, he stopped and smiled.

"So here we are at last. You look just like him. Your grandfather was a great friend of mine and my first disciple in this place. I must confess, yes, confession is good for the soul," he laughed, as he made the sign of the cross and spat on the floor. "I told you a small lie this morning. My name is not Thomas Gilychrist. It is Richard Gilychrist, but then I think that you know that already. Your grandmother told me everything while you slept. I am afraid she couldn't be here with us tonight and well, after a little chat about old times, I cut her throat with this," he said, pulling a sharp curved dagger from amongst his robes. Jonah let out a roar, a scream of fury that resounded in the cathedral of his mind, and tried with all his might to throw himself at the devil Gilychrist. He was transfixed, only a single drop of sweat running down his brow gave any sign of the gargantuan struggle within.

"She wasn't as pretty as when I last saw her. Did she ever tell you what I did to her? Did she tell you she hated it? She fucking loved it!" Gilychrist hissed in Jonah's ear, his foul breath washing over his face. "She squirmed like a whore. I had to throw her from the church the next morning, like Christ with the money lenders. She couldn't get enough," he said laughing. "But that is all in the past. Should I tell you what happened next? Should I tell you how your treacherous father failed in his mission, how he lied to himself for all those years, telling himself that I was dead, burnt and gone forever? Well, I was burned but not gone. I escaped below through the tunnels. I had the entrance to the tunnels hidden beneath the wooden altar of the church. As I ran down the stone steps, deep underground, my skin blackening and peeling, the pain was exquisite. A living thing when I hit the bottom, I threw myself into the dark waters of the lake, expecting to die but the noise above, the scent of blood and burning flesh became a fitting sacrifice for those who slept in the depths of the lake. I had awoken the dreamers and they, his disciples raised me up and, through his magic, I was healed and became his follower, until it was time to come to the surface once again, here to this place with my brothers. Here," he said, grabbing one of the robed figures and dragging it near. "Here, look in wonder and behold the face of your new gods!"

Without another word, he turned and grabbed the other man's cowl and snatched it down. The creature was beyond description, its skin was slime covered and its large eyes were like blobs of white jelly. Its skull was sleek and misshapen and its mouth lipless, wide and filled with row after row of small razor sharp teeth. It flinched away from Gilychrist's torch and croaked at him in anger, before quickly raising its hood and shambling away. Jonah realised in horror that the creature's hands were webbed, the long fingers tipped with black spear like claws.

He prayed to faint, to be released from the terror inside, but it was no good. His body was not his own, he belonged to the denizens of whatever hell waited below.

Suddenly, Gilychrist threw up his hands and in a booming voice began to chant. The robed figures dropped to their knees, raised their hands in supplication and joined in the chorus. " Yog gro shanack ento ekla shall gra," they chanted into the night. "Mel shall gra tak cla." The ground shifted under Jonah's feet and a great spout of water shot up into the air from the night darkened well.

Gilychrist turned, his face suffused with a hateful triumph. Moving forward, he raised the sacrificial knife.

"Behold," he screeched into the night. "The sleeper has awoken." The last thing that Jonah saw as the blade was dragged across his throat was a great worm erupting from the well. A thousand blind eyes covered its segmented body as it bellowed its triumph into a night sky that fell like a blanket over the accursed village of Homestead.

JOE'S TALE

Jeffery Donovan stepped off the train at St Austell, stuffing his mobile phone back in his pocket before quickly hurrying to the taxi rank outside. He jumped in the nearest car, dragging his bag in beside him before telling the driver in clipped tones that he was heading for Mevagissey. The driver, perhaps sensing his haste, merely nodded his head and pulled out of the station, as Jeffery fumbled his phone out of his coat pocket before once again hitting the speed dial for home.

The phone rang maddeningly over and over again and yet there was still no answer. Cursing quietly, he cancelled the call and tried David and Jenny's house across the road. They weren't only neighbours but good friends of the family but there was no answer there either.

It had been three days, now, since Jeffery had last heard from his wife and children. In that time, he had tried to ring them hundreds of times, all to no avail. The last time he and Tricia had talked, they had finally reconciled and he had agreed to come back home. She had promised to ring him back the very next day as it was getting late and the kids needed to go to bed. After another five minutes of chatting to his daughters, where they both told him how much they missed and loved him and he himself openly crying, the call had ended with a hesitant love you from Tricia and a promise to call him back early the next day. But the call had never come.

He had waited patiently all the next day, not wanting to call before she was ready, not wanting to seem too pushy or desperate. After all, he had fucked up big time and was now slinking back home like a dog with its tail tucked firmly between its legs after his month long banishment to his mother's house.

Around six thirty in the evening, he had finally caved in and rung, wanting to speak to the children before their bed time, but there had been no answer. This in itself was strange. Trish was a creature of habit. Already on any normal evening, the girls would be in their pyjamas by now, their teeth cleaned and ready for a couple of stories before bed. But the phone rang on and on.

After his third or fourth try, he tried Trish's mobile, but still nothing. After a moment's thought, he gave it up and decided to try again after dinner. But the result had been the same, no answer. He tried again every hour, on the hour, till nine o'clock, before calling David and Jenny but there had been no answer their either. This actually put his mind at ease somewhat. Perhaps Trish had taken the kids out with David and Jenny and their two little boys maybe to Play Palace or perhaps just down to the village park. After all, it was still early autumn and the nights warm and barmy, and there was no rule to say the kids had to be in bed bang on seven o'clock every night. Nevertheless, he tried Trish's mobile once again, just to be sure, and got no reply.

Frowning, he placed the phone back down into the receiver, just a little too hard, earning a raised eyebrow from his mother who shuffled past in her slippers, a steaming cup of tea in her hand as she headed into the sitting room to watch the evening news. Sighing, knowing he was going to get twenty questions, he followed her in and tried to watch the news. He tried to ring Trish and Jenny's house twice more before sending Trish an email asking her to ring him first thing in the morning. Finally, he went to bed but his sleep was troubled.

The next day was more of the same. He even went as far as to pull out the Yellow Pages and ring someone from the village at random but, after trying the numbers of eleven complete strangers and getting no answers, he gave it up and started looking on the internet for any news of power cuts in and around the Mevagissey area. After finding nothing, he went back online and booked a seat on the first train back to Cornwall the very next day.

Now, he sat in the back of taxi cab playing with his phone, rubbing it between his hands like a magical lamp only, instead of a genie, wishing for a call or even a text, anything to let him know his family was ok.

"Quiet today." Jeffery looked up from his musing.

"Sorry," he mumbled.

"The village," the cabbie said. "Quiet today." Jeffery looked up, startled to see they were pulling into his very street. "Just say where," the cabbie said, nodding towards the silent houses.

"Just here will do," Jeffery said, reaching into his pocket for his wallet. He paid the driver a twenty and told him to keep the change. The cabbie thanked him kindly then sped away without a backward glance. Jeffery started up his path, noticing the car was parked in the drive then suddenly stopped. Something was wrong. It was quiet, almost too quiet. In fact, it was dead silent. Not a seagull screeched in the sky, no laughing children could be heard from the nearby park, not even a Sunday lawnmower was running. He wanted to see somebody, anybody, but especially Trish, Trish and the kids, anything to squash this sense of foreboding.

Reaching for the door, he pushed the handle, half expecting it to be locked but it wasn't and the door swung open easily.

"Trish," he called, stepping inside and dropping his bag. "Debbie, Lucy?" Nothing. His word hung there, caught in silence. "Trish," he called again, popping his head into the living room before heading down the hall to the kitchen. "Girls, daddy's home."

The kitchen was neat, orderly and empty. He started to feel panic rise into his stomach, making him feel slightly queasy. He didn't stop but took several deep breaths as he headed for the stairs, trying to get his whirling emotions under control. He jogged up the stairs, starting to feel angry. Where the hell were they?

"Trish," he called again, quickly opening the girls' room. Nothing. Next, he headed for the room he and Trish had shared for the last ten years but it was empty too. In desperation, he even tried the bathroom but it was also empty, just like the rest of the house. Not waiting, he dashed down the stairs and headed across the road to David and Jenny's house. He was halfway down their garden path when he noticed the window. It was broken. Hell, that was too nice a word. It was smashed to shit, even the wooden frame was snapped and gouged. Jenny's fine white curtains billowed out through the shattered frame, flapping and tearing themselves on what was left of the splintered glass.

Jeffery stopped and licked his lips nervously. What the hell was going on here? It was like something from the fucking Twilight Zone. Furious, he marched up the garden path and, without even knocking, he stormed into the house. He wanted answers and he was going to get them, Goddammit.

He stopped dead. The house was in chaos and, oh God, was that blood on the walls? His knees felt like jelly and his legs could no longer support him as with a groan he slumped against the door frame.

There was blood, blood everywhere, sprayed across the walls. Lakes of the stuff had soaked into the carpet. It had even burnt itself into the lightbulb. Suddenly, the smell seemed to be all about him. The smell of copper pennies held too long in a tight fist. Feeling his gorge rise, he turned and stumbled into the garden and threw up his lunch. Trembling, he stood up. Wiping his mouth with the back of his hand, he stumbled back inside.

"Jenny," he called. "David?" He couldn't just leave, even if he wanted to. What if they were hurt and where were the kids? "David, Goddammit," he called, trying to avoid the blood as he headed into the kitchen. "Where the hell are you?"

The kitchen was empty but a complete wreck. Every cupboard door had been torn open and the contents strewn all about the kitchen as if someone had been frantically searching for something. The upstairs was the same. In the bathroom, the medicine cabinet had been torn from the wall and the shower curtain shredded and torn down. The kids' room was the same. The blankets were ripped from the boys' beds, their toys strewn about and little Johnnie's fish tank smashed into a thousand pieces. Jeffery said a small prayer of thanks. There was no blood here, before going back onto the landing and heading for the master bedroom.

He was just about to turn the handle when the smell hit him. It was the smell of long dead ocean, of rotting seaweed and decaying fish. It seemed to be crawling from under the door, floating through the keyhole and seeping from the very pores of the door itself. Raising an arm to cover his nose, he turned the handle and pushed his way into the room. He stopped dead, his hands dropping away from his face, his eyes widening as he took in the chaos within.

There were dead things everywhere: octopus, squid, fish, all rotten and bloated. Seaweed covered the smashed furniture, covering the carpet, splattered up the walls and hanging from the ceiling in great strands. Both David and Jenny lay on the bed, covered in the loathsome weed. As he watched on in horror, a large crab pushed its way from between Jenny's tattered lips and scurried down her chest. A scream building in his throat, he backed out of the room then bolted down the stairs, stumbling and falling, crashing into the wall. He turned and ran out the door and into the street.

He was in a full blown panic now, screaming his wife's name, calling for his children as he hammered on doors and banged windows, looking for someone, anyone.

He was halfway down the Vandraven driveway when he pulled up short, the house looming above him, acting like a hard slap to the face bringing him back to senses. No one was here. Nobody ever came here. If ever there was a haunted house, a truly haunted house, the Vandraven House was it.
Backing down the driveway, he turned and headed down the hill towards the harbour, throwing nervous glances over his shoulder till he crested the hill and the old house was safely out of sight.

Below him was the village harbour. Usually, it would be bustling with life as Cornish fishermen unloaded the day's catch, cleaned their boats and mended their nets. But now, there was nothing. Not a person stirred. The only sound the gentle lapping of waves and the cry of a lone seagull circling overhead.

He was just about to start down and investigate further when he noticed movement out of the corner of his eye. There was a small boat out to sea floundering, engine smoking as it spluttered its way towards a small shingle covered beach just left of the local lighthouse. Jeffery felt a pang in his heart as he remembered many a sun soaked day spent playing on that very beach with his children, their laughter and screeches of delight as they paddled and swam in the cold waters. He had to find them to find out what was going on here, to get some answers!

Quickly, he ran down the hill onto the harbour side, passed rocking boats and silent shops. Here, there were more dead creatures and crawling seaweed but he barely noticed as he ran on towards the deserted beach. He could hear the boat's engine now, spluttering, failing. Hurrying passed the lighthouse, he descended the stone steps, taking two at a time until he hit the beach and waded into the freezing waters up to his waist. Grabbing onto the now drifting boat, he hauled it into the shallows until it run aground.

There was a man inside, lying face down in a puddle of water. Quickly, Jeffery scrambled aboard. Grabbing the man by the shoulders, he hauled him over. It was Joe, Joe Thomas, a good friend of David and Jenny's and a sometimes acquaintance of his own. Joe was a fisherman from a long line of fishermen who had lived and fished the surrounding waters for generations. Usually he was a big man, with a round smiling face, but now he was a shadow of his former self, his face sunken, his body wasted and emaciated. His breath was shallow and foul as he struggled to breathe from between dry, parched lips.

"Water," he begged, his hands pawing weekly at Jeffery's arm. "Please, for the love of God, water."

"I have none, Joe," he replied, grasping the other man's hand. "I am sorry, I have none. What's happened here, Joe? Where is everyone? Where is Tricia and the children? Please, Joe," he begged, "you have to help me find them."

"Gone," Joe whispered. "All gone. They took them, took them to punish us."

"Who?" Jeffery grabbed at him. "Who has them, Joe? Who has my children?"

"Gone," Joe repeated. "All gone. Not just your family, everyone. They took them down into the deep. It was our fault, all our fault, but we didn't know. How could we know?"

"What is it? What are you talking about?" Jeffery asked, tempted to give the other man a shake, but not quite daring to do so.

"This," Joe gasped, opening his fist. There was a flash of gold as something clattered into the bottom of the boat. Reaching down, Jeffery picked up the fallen object and stared at it in disbelief. It was some kind of idol, no doubt about that. An idol carved out of solid gold but like nothing he had ever seen before. Whatever creature it was meant to represent, he had never seen before. He could only describe it as octopus like in nature, yet completely outside of nature with its many tentacle like arms and great staring eyes. It fascinated and repulsed him all at the same time.

"Where did you get this, Joe?" he said, managing to drag his eyes away from it. "Where in God's name did you get this?"

"Out there," he gasped, his eyes rolling towards the ocean. "We was trawling past Chapel Point when our nets became tangled. We managed to get them free and bring them up, the crane smoking and trembling under the strain. When they surfaced, they was filled with large stones, blocks. They had pictures on them like them old temples you see in Egypt."

"Hieroglyphics," Jeffery murmured. "You're talking about hieroglyphics."

"Yes," Joe said, scrabbling at his arm once again. "Hieroglyphics and those things, hundreds of them amongst the rocks and seaweed, all shapes and sizes. Gold! Solid gold! We took them back to the village, my brothers and I, and hid them away until we could decide what to do with them. But they came for them, those things, came in the storm from the sea, came to take them back and to take the people with them down into the cold, into the deep. But I fooled them," he chuckled, weakly. "I hid in the one place I knew they wouldn't look, in their own back yard out there on the sea. They will come again, tonight. They always come at night. Can't stand the clean light of day. It must be dark where they come from, so very dark. You have to give it back to them, Jeff, you have to give it back to them." For a moment, his grip tightened almost painfully then fell away as the light faded from his eyes and he breathed his last desperate breath.

Jeffery sat there for some time, staring at the thing in his hand and waited. Just as the sun started to sink in the West, he clambered out of the boat and knelt on the beach, holding the golden idol towards the sea. As darkness fell, he closed his eyes and prayed to whatever gods might be listening and waited.

After what seemed like an eternity, he heard a splash of water and crunching on the gravel before him. Suddenly, his skin began to crawl and the hair on the back of his neck stood to attention.

He could feel its presence, now, looming over him, something ancient, a dweller from the deep, an outsider, something beyond the understanding of men. He could feel its animosity and a cold hatred radiating from it in waves, causing him to break out in a cold sweat as an icy hand closed over his own.

He nearly fainted then at the feel of that terrible hand. It felt like nothing more than bone covered in cold jelly, yet it radiated a terrible heat, then it was gone and the idol with it.

For a moment, he was tempted to open his eyes, until he felt the creature's frigid breath upon his neck.

"Do not look at me," the creature gurgled as if reading his mind. "Do not look at me." At the sound of that terrible voice, he fainted away, only to awaken once again with the coming dawn.

The creature was gone, the idol was gone and so was Joe. He knew where they were now, his family, and knew he must follow.

Stripping off his clothes, he waded into the freezing waters, feeling it instantly sap his strength as it crashed over his legs, his waist, his chest. When a cold hand wrapped around his ankle, he opened his mouth to scream and the ocean rushed in, filling his body with dark waters.

SEATED

"Shit!" Jason Burnett shouted, sticking his thumb in his mouth. He had been working on a particularly nasty blackberry patch when a large hand had fallen heavily on his shoulder, causing him to jerk in surprise and rake his hands amongst the waiting thorns. He turned, meaning to rain down curses on the offending person but the words died on his lips when he saw to whom the offending hand belonged.

Jason didn't know the man by name but he had seen him strolling about the tattered tents and rusting caravans that had suddenly appeared with the coming of the gypsies. He wasn't exactly hard to miss. The man must have stood nearly seven feet tall with a mane of flowing black hair streaked with silver. He wore a large gold hoop in his left ear but it was the scars that the eyes were most drawn to. The man's face was a mass of scars, the worst running from the top of his forehead all the way passed the empty socket of his left eye and petering at the bottom of his stubble covered chin.

It was this terrible wound that Jason Burnett was trying to drag his eyes away from when the man began to speak.

"We have come to help you with your festival," he said in a strange accent revealing broken, blackened teeth. Jason winced, trying not to recoil as the reek of stale tobacco washed over him.

"You mean Feast Week," he replied somewhat bemused.

"Yes," the man said, flashing his rotting teeth. "Just so, we have come to help you with your Feast Week."

"Sorry, it's volunteers only and we cannot pay you for your trouble." At this, the other man straightened, his bushy eyebrows crushing together.

"Did I mention money, town man? Always there is mistrust between men from town and the travelling folk. I offer help only to show goodwill and to thank you for letting us stay, if only for a little while." Jason, who was head of the village committee and who was working furiously with the local authorities to roust the gypsies out of the village before the start of Feast Week, could only smile weekly and offer a non-to-sincere apology.

"I am sorry, my friend," he said, holding up a restraining hand, "not many people even here in the village want to do such tiresome labour on a hot sunny day and especially for free, so you understand my misgivings."

"Of course," the big man smiled, taking a step back. Jason noticed, however, that the man's smile never quite reached his eyes and he realised in that moment that not only did he dislike this man but he feared him a little too. "So it's decided," the gypsy continued, holding out a large nicotine stained hand. Jason reached for the hand but was grasped by the forearm instead. "My name is Radak Lulpine. I am king among the travelling folk." For a moment, Jason was tempted to bow and call the other man your majesty but considered it unwise and simply introduced himself as Jason Burnett.

His mind was racing now a mile a minute. It was already late May and the tourists had started a slow but steady trickle into the village. The last thing that Jason and the rest of the village council needed was a bunch of scruffy looking gypsies hanging round the village square or stinking up the harbour with its picturesque lighthouse and outstanding views of St Austell Bay. Luckily, they had decided to camp on the back fields of School Hill, far from the centre of the village, which gave Jason Burnett an idea. There was a coastal path nearby, leading from Mevagissey to nearby Pentewan. At this time of year, the path would be overgrown with nettles brambles and tall wild grasses. He would put the gypsies to work clearing the path. This would serve two purposes: one, it would keep them close to their own encampment and, two, would keep them busy just long enough for Jason to convince the local authorities to roust them out of the village.

Smiling, Jason took the other man's arm. "Let's talk."

It was early the following evening as Jason was enjoying a well-deserved pint after a busy day of erecting flags and laying bunting when John Stampton barged into the lantern. He didn't look about, just hurried across the room to where Jason sat at the bar. His face was flushed and Jason noticed the other man's shirt was drenched with sweat as if he'd come on the run.

"Whatever is the matter?" he asked, turning to more readily face the other man. For a moment, John Stampton said nothing but just stood there, puffing and panting, as he tried to catch his breath. His first words, however, turned Jason's blood cold.

"The Vandraven House."

"What about it?" Jason asked, hopping off his stool.

"I saw them hanging around up there."

"What!" Jason exclaimed a little too loudly before grasping the other man's shoulder and hustling him outside. "What the fuck are they doing up there and why didn't you move them along?"

"I didn't feel like I had the right," John squirmed.

"You're part of the village council, John, same as me, and you know it."

"I know it," John said, not quite able to meet the other man's eyes. "And I ain't afraid of a few gypsies if that's what you're thinking. It's that damn house, Jason. I ain't going anywhere near that place."

Jason sighed, his shoulders slumping.

"Alright, John. I will go up there and take care of it but don't go shooting your mouth off. The last thing I need is people from the village getting wind that those people are rummaging round up there."

"Ok, Jason," the other man said, almost fawningly, as Jason turned and headed up the hill. "But we need to get them away from that house," he called after him. Jason didn't turn, just raised a hand in salute and headed on his way.

Ten minutes later, he was heading down Beach Road passed the well-kept houses towards the coastal path. The Vandraven House was at the end of the row, a little apart from the rest of the houses. A large manor estate surrounded by its own grounds, it sat facing the cold waters of the Atlantic like some dark sentinel from another time. Built in 1835 by Lucas Vandraven, the house was a place of murder, suicide and madness, a dark blot, a stain on the village, cursed and shunned by all and now the God damn gypsies were mooching around up there. Jason just hoped and prayed they hadn't somehow managed to find a way inside because he sure as shit wasn't going in after them.

He was there now, just passing the old place, when he heard voices coming from around the back of the house that bordered on the coastal path. He hurried on a little faster, listening intently. There were voices alright coming from a crumbling piece of wall that led onto the Vandraven grounds and one of them was definitely the voice of a small child. That decided him, the Vandraven estate was no place for children, or anybody else for that matter.

Cursing, he boosted himself up onto the wall and just stopped, his mouth agape. Part of the garden had been completely cleared away. It stood out in stark contrast to the overgrown trees, thorn bushes and general neglect of the rest of the grounds. Jason was just about hop down and march over to where a group of gypsies stood gathered about, their backs towards him, when Radak Lulpine suddenly appeared in front of him like some evil jack in the box.

"My friend," he exclaimed, leaping on the wall, driving Jason backwards. He would have taken a nasty tumble if Radak had not landed beside him, gripping his shoulder in one massive arm. Jason shook the other man off angrily. Stepping away, he straightened his shirt with quick angry jerks.

"What the hell are you doing in there?" he demanded, his anger overriding his fear of the bigger man.

"What you asked us to do," Radak replied, ignoring the anger in the other man's voice. "Look," he said, walking quickly towards Jason, both arms outstretched. Jason had no choice but to retreat further down the path away from the Vandraven House. "You see," Radak said, nodding over Jason's shoulder. Jason turned reluctantly and glanced down the path but quickly turned back.

"Very good," he said, not so easily distracted.

"Yes," Radak beamed, "my people have been working very hard."

"You didn't answer my question," Jason interrupted. "What are you doing at the Vandraven House?" Radak sighed as if bored with the whole conversation.

"My friend, what harm has been done? Yes, yes, I know that perhaps this place is the private property but it is old and long abandoned. The grounds were a mess and clearly visible along the path from behind the crumbling walls, so I told my people to clean the place a little so you will see how hard the people of Radak work for your village! Tell me, my friend, how have we offended you?" Jason felt his anger evaporate, leaving him feeling small and petty. The gypsies had done a damn fine job of clearing the path and what they had done to the Vandraven grounds had been almost fucking miraculous.

It was the house, the God damn house. It got under your skin, into your psyche, and Jason began to wonder if madness was catching.

"I am sorry, Radak," he said, offering a sincere apology, "but you shouldn't be in that place. It is dangerous. The house is old and many bad things have happened there." A sudden voice piped from behind the stone wall, speaking in a language Jason did not understand. Radak's reaction was immediate as he scurried to the wall, leaving Jason hanging in mid conversation. He reached down and scooped up a little girl. Jason guessed her age to be no older than seven or eight. She had flowing white hair and her eyes were covered with a filthy looking bandage. Nevertheless, when Radak placed her gently on the ground, she moved with a speed and grace that belied any form of handicap.

"The child is blind?" Jason asked as he watched her hurry away.

"Yes," Radak replied, his chest swelling with pride. "Even the least of Radak's people is a good worker, but it is of no mind. We look after our own, as we always have. You were saying about the house, it is dangerous? I am thinking you mean, old, how is it you say, unstable? It will collapse all about us?"

"Yes," Jason said, seizing upon the idea. It was as good an explanation as any and a damn sight easier to explain. "Yes," he said again, peering up at the old house. "This place is very old and should have been condemned many years ago. Besides, you have cleared the part of the grounds that can be seen from the path. No need to endanger your people any further."

"Quite right," Radak replied, turning back to the wall. He let out two short sharp whistles. Almost immediately, as if they had been poised there all along, the other gypsies began to scrabble over the walls, an assortment of rusty looking tools slung over their shoulders. Radak spat something at them in the same musical language the little girl had spoken and they hurried on a little faster. Radak waited until the last man was over then patted Jason on the shoulder and swiftly walked away.

Jason stood there and watched him go, before heading back to the village, trying hard not to glance at the Vandraven House as he passed. Still, he felt buried in its shadow as he hurried away.

The next two days passed in a blur of committee meetings, phone calls and long hours of general preparation as Feast Week loomed ever closer. Jason had just got off the phone and was contemplating a nice warm bath when there came a loud knock at the door. With a sigh, he crossed the hall and reluctantly opened the door.

John Stampton stood there, the setting sun blazing behind him, lending him an almost ethereal quality. Jason had not seen John since that day in The Lantern but here he was again and Jason had the sinking feeling he was once again the bearer of more bad news.

"There, up there again," he blurted. "Old Mary Fairweather saw them as she was walking her dogs along the coastal path, heard them, too, singing and carousing like they was having some kind of party."

"Son of a bitch," Jason exclaimed, slamming the door behind him. "I told them to stay the fuck out of there." John was just about to reply when Jason turned on him, grabbing him by the arm. "You're coming with me this time, John. You're just as much a committee member as I am. Maybe they will listen to you. They sure as shit ain't listening to me."

"Ok, ok, ease up, Jason, for Christ's sake. I am coming along, ain't I," John said, shaking free. Jason let him go, mumbling and cursing to himself as the other man fell in beside him, sullenly rubbing at his wrist.

Neither man spoke to the other until they had traversed the harbour, crested School Hill and hit Beach Road. There, they stopped, watching as the sun began its slow descent into the sea, lending the Vandraven House a kind of blood hew glow.

"Let's get this done," Jason said, squaring his shoulders. "I don't want to be anywhere near this place in the dark."

"So, what's the plan?" John asked in a small voice. Jason Burnett was his friend, and the man had a big heart, but it was best to tread carefully round him when his temper was up.

"I will tell you what I am going to do," he said, setting off at pace. "I am going to tell them to get the fuck out of there. That smooth talking son of a bitch lied to me."

"Ok," John said, hurrying to keep up, "but maybe best not to go in there screaming and shouting. Hey, Jason, we don't want to upset anybody." The thought of shouting and screaming at Radak Lulpine made his balls feel tight and uncomfortable. If Jason heard him, he gave no sign, just kept on going with his head down, muttering to himself. He was tired and pissed off, and could do without all the extra hassle. He would tell Lulpine to get the hell off the grounds and threaten him with the law if he ever came back. Enough was enough, Goddammit.

The shadows had just started to seriously lengthen by the time they arrived at the crumbling section of wall where Radak's party had last entered the Vandraven grounds, and once again Jason could hear voices coming from the other side. He was about to start clambering over when two burley looking gypsies suddenly emerged from the shadows. They were both big men, not as big as Radak Lulpine, but far from small fry either and, for some reason, they were both wearing rather unpleasant smiles, smiles that made Jason Burnett feel very uncomfortable.

He was just about to ask where the hell Radak was when a large fist came crashing out of the darkness and he went away for a little while.

He did not come out of the darkness gradually but snapped awake, the sound of screaming piercing the dark vale of unconsciousness. He tried to stand, to focus, but was dragged back down into a seated position, his arms cruelly twisted up his back. It was nearly full dark now and the Vandraven estate was lit by flickering torches.

John Stampton was being dragged towards some kind of stone altar. No, that was wrong, not an altar but a chair, a kind of stone throne that sat facing the ocean, the last rays of the setting sun blazing across its cold waters. The poor man was stark naked and covered in blood. Runic like symbols had been carved into his quivering flesh. He screamed again, the terrified shriek of a trapped animal, but the gypsies, dragging him along, only laughed at his feeble efforts to escape.

Jason, seeing his friend's fate, began to struggle, but was held easily in place by his captor's enormous strength. He only realised it was Radak himself who held him captive when the man began to whisper into his ear.

"Now you shall see something, town man, a ceremony that has not been held for a thousand years."

"Why are you doing this?" Jason stammered.

"Because it needs to be done. Once this place was ours and belonged to our people, a sacred place. But that was before the Romans came with their false gods and scattered the people, burning our sacred places. Then, after them, the disciples of the Lamb God, Jesus, who killed our priest and converted the people with their lies and false promises of heaven, until only a few of our sacred places remained. This was one of these places, or at least it was until that monstrosity was built," he said, nodding towards the Vandraven House. "Our oracle tells us that the sacred stones that once sanctified this place were destroyed, crushed and used in the very foundations of that terrible house, and you wonder why it is cursed," he snorted. But Jason barely heard a word. He only had eyes for the tableaux unfolding before him.

John Stampton had mercifully passed into unconsciousness. This seemed to bother the surrounding gypsies not one bit as they flung his bleeding body into the crumbling throne and secured his hands and feet to its ruined frame with bits of rope and fraying twine.

"See, she comes," Radak hissed from behind him, just as a small girl appeared from the shadows. She stood alone, dressed in a pure white robe. The stark white bandages wrapped about her eyes shone like a halo and Jason recognised her as the blind girl he had seen move with such eerie grace only a couple of days before.

As he watched on, the girl savagely ripped the bandages from her face. The surrounding gypsies gave out a collective sigh. Jason, however, began to scream. He screamed long and loud until, cursing, Radak managed to stuff a sweat stained rag deep into his mouth.

"Silence, town man," he hissed. "Your time to scream will come soon enough." But Jason couldn't help it. The girl's face was terrifyingly alien. Both her eyes were white with cataracts, except for the third which sat in the middle of her forehead, just above the bridge of her nose. This eye was black and pupiless. As Jason watched on, his screams ignored, it began to ooze blood that ran down her face like crimson tears.

"Radak," the girl snapped. "Bring me the knife." Radak quickly signalled to another man and, for just a split second, Jason was free, before another strong pair of hands clamped him down. Radak meanwhile had scurried across the clearing and was down on one knee, offering up the sacrificial knife to the waiting girl. She took it from him reverently, chanting in her small voice until the rest of the gypsies joined in, defiling the night with their guttural singing.

As the girl approached the stone chair, the chanting increased, becoming wild and untamed. Some of the gypsies began to convulse, lost in the ecstasy of the moment. Others fell to their knees, tears running down their faces. The girl raised her hand and the crowd fell immediately silent.

She was up on the chair now, standing on the seat between John's splayed legs, knife poised above his throat. She muttered something, an incantation or perhaps some kind of prayer. Either way, the moment the words left her lips, John's eyes flew open. He had time for one last terrible scream before she brought the knife flashing down, slashing him deep across the throat, rupturing arteries and tearing through sinew. Blood began to spurt and she flung herself backwards into Radak's waiting arms. She immediately struggled free and fell to her knees, taking up her terrible chanting once again.

Jason felt his bladder let go as the chair began to vibrate then smoke. Eventually, the stone started to melt, run and crawl, adhering to John's poor dead body, dissolving him, eating him, making him a part of the whole until he was completely gone and the chair sat there, renewed and revitalised.

The girl stood, bloody knife in hand, and the gypsies went wild, cheering, surging forward and falling at her feet. As she approached the swaying Jason, Radak stood proudly by her side. Jason's eyes went wide with terror as he saw the bloody knife still clenched in her small fist. She followed his gaze and smiled.

"Not to worry, town man. The knife is not for you, though you will feel its bite many times before the night is through. At times, you will wish for death, even beg for it, for pain is as much a sacrifice as any death."

"Radak," she said, handing him the bloody knife. "Shall we begin?"

The sun was just starting to stain the night sky when Jason Burnett was placed upon the throne. He had endured hours of torture at the hands of his captors. Just like the girl had said, he had begged them to kill him as they carved the ancient runes and symbols of the summoning into his bleeding flesh.

At one point, he had begun to ram the back of his head into the ground, desperate to escape the pain, but the gypsies had held him in place with ropes and strong hands, ignoring his pleas. He had screamed and begged for help but nobody had come. The night was eerily silent, as if some kind of spell had been cast over the whole village.

The night went on and on, perhaps a hundred years, maybe a thousand, until at last it was over.

Now he lay a bloody heap in the great stone chair, the sea stretching out before him as infinite as the sky. By his side stood the girl, her robes stained with his blood. Before her stood Radak, knife in hand. At some unseen signal, he took up a place behind her as she knelt in the dirt. Facing the sea, she began to chant, her voice booming, bouncing off the nearby cliffs as she took Jason's hand, their fingers entwining, her cries becoming frantic, now pleading, beckoning. In front of them, the dark waters of the Atlantic began to heave and stir.

The girl let out a scream of triumph as she raised their entwined hands into the air. This was the signal Radak had been waiting for and, without a moment's hesitation, he plunged the sacred knife through the girl's neck, killing her instantly before turning the knife upon himself.

Jason could feel himself slipping away now, blood loss and shock taking him down into blessed death. The last thing his fading vision beheld was a huge monolith rising from the sea. Something clung to its side, something unspeakable, something reaching towards him.

He found the strength for one last scream before darkness drew him under.

In the predawn light, a figure arose from the stone chair. Its skin was flawless and it wore the face of Jason Burnett. It stood facing the Vandraven House for some time. As the sun rose in the East, it stepped into the house's shadow then disappeared inside.

BROKEN MESSIAH

He sat cleaning his weapons and tried his best to ignore his own reflection. It wasn't easy. The room was small and dingy with a single bed, bathroom and not much else. The mirror was bolted to the back of the door and reflected the entire room. He glanced up again, a moth drawn to a burning flame. This time, he did not look away from the stranger glaring back at him. Raising his hand, he slowly ran it over the mass of scar tissue that used to be his face. Only the eyes remained whole and untouched, green and wild with the atrocities he had committed in the name of God. Dropping his hand to his throat, he let his fingers trail over the ruined flesh, scarred by tooth and claw, down further over the broad expanse of his chest. Here, the scars were faded and white with age. These had been his first, the first of many more to come in a life of pain and violence that spanned nearly thirty years.

He dropped his eyes back to his weapons and continued with the oiling, stripping and cleaning. This was an old ritual for him, perhaps his own fucked up version of meditation. If this was so, it wasn't working today. Cursing, he fitted the last parts of his weapons together and headed for the bathroom. With rough, jerky movements, he stripped off his clothes and flung them in the corner before stepping in the shower, eager to wash away the cold sweat that seemed to cover every inch of his body. After a while, the steamy warm water began to do its job and he began to relax. With a sigh, he rotated his neck, releasing the tension as he began to wash himself down.

He was a big man, nearly six and a half feet, with a large frame heavily corded with muscle. His hair was a black mop just starting to show the first hints of grey. As an orphan boy, he had grown up with the church and had turned into a handsome youth but that had been before the training, the missions and the scars. Almost unconsciously, he dropped his hands to the deep wounds that ran across his chest. Out of all the creatures he had hunted and killed, it had been the church that had wounded him the deepest and, in doing so, had not only saved his life but also his immortal soul. Thousands of blood soaked nights had passed since that terrible night and, although he had only been a small child, he remembered it completely.

It had been late that night when his father had finally returned home, his mood as black as the dark mud that stuck to his boots and streaked his damp trousers. With a grunt, he slammed the door closed against the night and kicked off his muddy boots before cracking open his shotgun across his arm, removing the gleaming shells and locking both away. Only after he had shrugged out of his heavy jacket did he notice a young Johnny sitting on the stairs, snug and warm in his Thomas the Tank Engine pyjamas, Pooh Bear clamped in one tiny fist. At first, a flash of annoyance had crossed his father's face then he gave a rueful smile and ruffled the boy's hair.

"You're up late, Johnny. Isn't it time you was in bed, lad?"

"He wanted to wait up for you," his mother said from across the room where she sat by a crackling fire, a basket of knitting in her lap. "Did you see anything?"

"Perhaps," his father replied, scooping Johnny up and taking a seat across from his wife, happy for the flickering fire's warmth.

"Perhaps?" his mother repeated.

"Shadows," his father said, looking troubled for a moment. "I thought I saw a shape, a dog perhaps."

"That would explain a lot," she said, winding up a ball of pink wool. "All those dead sheep, a wild dog pack maybe. You probably scared them away for the night. A few fence repairs and a couple of nights with the sheep locked safely away in the barn should set things to right."

"And if not?" his father asked, lighting his pipe.

"Then a few more nights out in the cold for you. Oh, don't look so cross," she chuckled. "I will pack you a flask of soup and you can wear your thermal underpants." Even Johnny got to laughing at that one. His father was just about to reply when there came a sharp knock on the door.

His father stood up, gently setting Johnny down on the living-room rug before glancing at the clock on the mantel piece. It was half past ten on a Thursday night on a quiet country road, not exactly the right time for neighbours to come calling. Glancing at his wife with a shrug, he headed for the door.

His father had just turned the latch when the door flew open and a naked man fell through the doorway, collapsing in a boneless heap upon the living room floor. The man was completely naked and covered from head to toe in blood.

"Jesus Christ," his father shouted, quickly kneeling by the man's side and gently turning him over.

"Help me," the man croaked.

"Where are you hurt? Sweet Jesus, you're covered in blood."

"Blood," the man growled, his voice suddenly stronger. "Yes, blood," he said, his eyes fixing on Johnny's father. "But not mine." Suddenly, his hand shot out, grabbing him by the throat as he effortlessly flowed to his feet, throwing his father across the room in one fluid motion, sending him crashing into the wall with bone numbing force.

Johnny's mother screamed and scooped up her knitting needles before jumping in front of the crying Johnny.

"What are you going to do with those, bitch?" the man growled. "Knit me to death?" Suddenly, the man started to change. His body seemed to grow longer, taller. His hands twisted and danced by his side as his fingers elongated, razor sharp claws shearing through his fingertips in an explosion of blood and shredded flesh. But it was the man's face that Johnny couldn't look away from. As he watched on, the man's face began to change, his nose flattening, his jaw growing heavy, as razor sharp teeth burst through his gums, filling his mouth with blood where it drooled down his chin, matting in the coarse black hair that now covered his entire body. Johnny's mother had time to let out a single ear-piercing shriek before her mind crumbled in terror and she fell hard to the floor in a dead faint.

For a moment, the creature just stood there, its blood filled mouth agape before bursting into a growling gibbering laughter. Suddenly, it stopped its obscene chuckling and fell on all fours, slowly slouching its way towards Johnny.

"What will you do now, little chicken?" the thing snarled. Johnny felt his bladder let go as he took a step towards the open door, hot piss running down his leg. The creature's eyes flicked in the direction of the open doorway then back to Johnny, pinning him in place. Suddenly, it moved in a blur of motion, slashing at Johnny's chest, shredding his clothes and leaving burning lines in the flesh beneath. With a cry, he staggered backward, clutching at his bleeding chest, calling out his father's name.

"Too late for him, boy," the creature said. "I can already smell him starting to rot. This one, however," it grinned, running a razor tipped finger up his mother's denim clad thigh, "is very much alive. Do you know what I am going to do to your precious mummy, boy? I am going to fuck her, fuck her until she begs me to stop then I am going to fuck her some more and, when I am finished, I am going to tear out her throat and eat her up just like the big bad wolf at granny's house."

"Please," Johnny begged but the creature just laughed.

"Too late for that, boy, but I will tell you what I will do. I shall let you run while I entertain your mother. After all, there is nothing like a good chase to burn off the night's excess. Run!" the thing howled, springing forward. "Run before I change my mind." With a scream, Johnny turned and ran. The last thing he saw as he fled into the night was the creature ripping at his mother's clothes.

The rest was a nightmare of tearing branches and cold sucking mud as he ran through the forest under the sailing light of a silvered moon. Crying, exhausted and bleeding, he finally staggered onto the roadside and collapsed into merciful darkness.

He awoke sometime later, wrapped in a coarse blanket, being carried in strong arms, the steeple of St Antony's looming out of the darkness. He began to struggle and cry out.

"Stop that, boy. Be thankful in His mercy that I found you when I did. If we hurry, there may still be time!" Johnny stopped his struggling at once as he recognised the voice of Father Peter, the parish priest.

"My mother," he sobbed. "There was a man."

"There are men coming to take care of your mother, Johnny," the priest said, unlocking the church door and quickly stepping inside. He set Johnny down on a nearby pew and locked the door behind them. "We should be safe now," he breathed, leaning heavily against the door. "Those things can't enter the house of God." That said, he turned and scooped Johnny up before rushing through the small church and into the back rooms that were his living quarters. There, he dropped Johnny into a ragged looking arm chair before disappearing through a curtained archway, returning only moments later carrying a small earthenware jar and a length of rope.

"Come on, boy," he said, pulling Johnny to his feet and dragging him back into the night darkened church. Releasing him, he lit a few fat white candles and positioned them around the altar. "Come here, Johnny," he said, holding out his hand to the boy who was now crouching down behind a row of pews, the blanket wrapped tight about him like a second skin. "Come here," the priest repeated, a sweat breaking across his brow. "There is no time for such foolishness." But still Johnny would not come. This man seemed like a stranger to him. Gone was the smiling Father Peter who ruffled his hair as he left the Sunday sermon with his mum and dad. In his place was this coarse stranger who shoved and pushed and cared nothing about a small boy's tears.

"Listen now," Father Peter said, edging closer towards the cowering boy. "Listen carefully, Johnny. You are in grave danger, not only your body but your very soul. The end of times is upon us and Satan's beast has marked you. We must purge you of this vileness before it is too late." Johnny had begun to back away as the priest came forward. Now he turned to run but it was too late. Father Peter lunged after him, grabbing him by the wrist and dragged him back towards the altar. Johnny went wild, kicking and screaming, struggling and biting.

"Forgive me, Johnny," Father Peter gasped as he crashed his fist into the boy's jaw. Stars exploded in Johnny's head and his knees unhinged. He was scooped up before he could hit the floor and was laid gently across the stone altar. He swam in the dark waters of unconsciousness until he felt the cruel burn of ropes digging into the scant flesh of his naked arms.

"What are you doing?" Johnny murmured, his vision sliding in and out of focus.

"I am sorry, Johnny, sorry for the pain I must cause you. One day you will understand and on that day I will beg your forgiveness but, until that day, we must travel a cruel road together." That said, he unscrewed the lid from the small jar Johnny had noticed earlier and dipped in his fingers before rubbing them experimentally under his nose. The smell hit Johnny in a wave of putrescence, causing his whole body to tremble and his stomach to roll and heave. Suddenly, he turned his head and nosily vomited onto the floor. Father Peter shook his head sadly.

"You see, Johnny, the wolf in you already tries to ascend. This is wolf's bane. It will help you. It will keep the wolf at bay until the others arrive." He dipped his finger back into the jar and, taking a deep breath, rubbed the ointment deep into the claw marks across Johnny's chest. The pain was unbelievable. A searing heat screamed through the wounds filling his mind, his world. He gave out a single ear-piercing scream then fell into blessed darkness.

He awoke sometime later to the sound of chanting, his body covered in sweat. He was still tied to the altar but there was no sign of Father Peter. Instead, three men stood about him. All were dressed in the vestment of the Priesthood but their faces were scarred and cruel. Suddenly, they stopped their chanting and another man stepped forward out of the shadows. He was dressed like the rest, apart from the thick leather gloves in which he held a small steaming chalice. The other men parted as the man came forward.

"This will cure you, boy, cure you or kill you. Either way, Lucifer will not have your soul this night."

"What are you doing?" Johnny tried to ask from between parched lips but the men looming above him had already started their vicious chanting, once again filling the small church with bastard Latin. The man in the gloves leaned over Johnny and, muttering a prayer, poured molten silver into Johnny's wounds.

He awoke two days later, a damp cloth pressed against his cracked lips. He sucked at the moisture greedily until it was gently taken away and used to softly wipe his face.

"You must wake up now, Johnny. You must grow strong for the days ahead." Johnny recognised the voice of Father Peter and his eyes flew open, his body twisting to get away, but the priest held him down firmly, but gently. "It's all right now, Johnny. No one will hurt you now. I am sorry for the pain you have endured but you were sick, poisoned, and we have made you well again. Now is a time for healing and reflection."

"My mother, my father?" Johnny asked, already knowing the answer but unable to grasp the concept in his tired child's mind.

"I am sorry, my son," Father Peter said, stroking the boy's tired brow, "but they are gone, gone to everlasting glory."

"You mean they're dead." The tears came easy now, hot and flowing down his face.

"Yes," Father Peter replied, shedding his own tears as he made the sign of the cross over Johnny's bed. "They were good people, your mother and father. They didn't deserve such a fate."

"What happened to them?" Johnny asked, trying to sit up. Father Peter tried to help him but pain shot through him and he sank back down with a groan, his hands pressed against his bandaged chest.

"It's too soon to talk of such things now, Johnny, for now you must eat, sleep and rest. When you are strong enough, we shall talk again."

The next two weeks passed in a blur for Johnny. He was mostly left alone with his grief and he slept a lot, only waking when Father Peter brought him his meals or came to change the tight bandages wrapped around Johnny's chest. The first time he had seen what was left of his chest he had vomited then fainted dead away. Now the great wounds were healing but the same could not be said for Johnny's mind. He still escaped his grief in the deep comfort of sleep and refused to get out of bed for any reason other than to use the bathroom. Even when Father Peter offered to take him outside for the first time in nearly two weeks, he still refused. This room, this bed, had become Johnny's refuge. To leave was to accept all that had happened to him and that Johnny refused to do.

Until, on the fifteenth day, all his options were taken from him. He awoke to the sound of raised voices then heavy footsteps on the stairs. His door was rudely pushed open. A man stood there, framed in the doorway. Johnny took one look at that scarred and terrible face and began to scream, then Father Peter was there holding him tight, crooning gentle words into his ear.

"You're scaring him, Matthew," Father Peter snapped at the other man. The man in the doorway ignored his words and looked round the room with disdain.

"You say he has not left these rooms in two weeks." The man's tone was accusatory as he turned to glare at Father Peter.

"I saved his life. Yes, saved his life and cared for him after you left him in a bed of pain."

"I would not have caused the boy any harm if it was not necessary. My men and I saved his soul and you know it, Peter."

"I know, old friend," Father Peter said, some of the anger leaving him, "but he is so young and already been through so much."

"And a long way to go yet," the other man said, sitting down at Johnny's feet slowly and carefully so as not to scare the boy. "I am Father Matthew. I can see by your face that you remember me. I am sorry for the pain I caused you but it was necessary for the sake of your soul that you were cleansed of that creature's filth."

"What was it?" Johnny asked in a small voice. The man seemed pleased by the boy's question but Father Peter shook his head sadly and turned away.

"It was a demon, Johnny, a Lycanthrope, a werewolf." Seeing the boy's confusion, he went on, "a man, a man possessed by a demon wolf you understand." But Johnny could only shake his head. He was a boy of eight brought up in a quiet rural community and knew nothing of such terrors until one had torn his life apart. Father Matthew, sensing some of the boy's thoughts, patted him gently on the knee and stood up, turning to Father Peter.

"I will return at seven pm sharp. I want him ready to leave, Peter. You have done all you can do for him. Now it is our turn to bring him closer to God." Father Peter said nothing, only nodded his agreement and left.

The other man lingered a moment longer, looking down at Johnny, his eyes searching, then he abruptly turned and walked away.

That evening found Johnny stood outside St Antony's, watching as the shadows grew deeper. Father Peter stood by his side, silent and unmoving. After what seemed like an eternity, a mud splattered Land Rover drew up beside them and Father Matthew clambered out. He did not speak but stood silently as Father Peter squatted down beside Johnny and turned the boy to face him.

"I am sorry I couldn't do more for you, Johnny," he said, plucking at the loose clothes that covered the boy's skinny frame. On that first night, he had burned what was left of Johnny's torn and bloody clothes, now the boy wore clothes salvaged from the church charity box, ill-fitting but warm and clean.

"You saved my life," Johnny said, shyly.

"I hope so, boy," Father Peter said, pulling him close for a hug, all the while looking up at the waiting Father Matthew. "I really hope I have." Standing abruptly, he ruffled the boy's hair. "Go with God, Johnny," he said before turning away and heading back inside. A large hand fell on Johnny's shoulder.

"Come on, boy," Father Matthew said, opening the passenger door for him. "We have a long way to go and time is fleeting." They drove all night, only stopping twice at the motorway services to use the bathroom and grab a couple of packs of stale sandwiches. Father Matthew spoke little and smoked a lot. He seemed unsettled, even uncomfortable in the presence of a child. Equally, Johnny felt small and scared in the presence of the big grim faced man.

At last, just as the first light of day started to stain the sky, they turned off onto a narrow country road and pulled in beside another couple of parked cars. Father Matthew climbed out and stretched before coming round to Johnny's side and ushered him out. They were on a cliff side overlooking the dark waters of the Atlantic. Behind them was a large copse of trees that hid a small hillock with a large metal door embedded in its side. As Johnny watched on, Father Matthew produced a bunch of metal keys from his coat pocket and unlocked the door. From over the big man's shoulder, Johnny could just see a set of narrow metal steps heading down into a poorly lit interior.

"Come on, boy," Father Matthew said, turning to Johnny and pointing down towards the stairs. "The others will be waiting for us." But Johnny would not move.

"Where are we and what is this place?"

"We are in Cornwall, Johnny," Father Matthew replied, taking him gently by the arm and nudging him forward. "And this is an old ammo bunker from the Second World War. It used to belong to the M.O.D. There was a gunnery range here once but the land belongs to the church now. Come along, now, no more questions. We still have much to do." Johnny knew it would be useless to delay any further and fell in behind Father Matthew as he descended the heavy metal stairs. The only sound was the echo of their foot falls and the fading sound of birdsong as they descended lower into the complex.

Suddenly, Father Matthew stopped in front of another metal door. Once again, out came the keys and the door was quickly opened. Inside was a chamber filled with old metal cots and wooden chairs piled into a corner against the rust streaked walls. Hurrying past these, they headed into a narrow corridor that branched off to the right, until they stood in front of another metal door. Here, Father Matthew stopped and sank down to one knee, facing Johnny.

"In this room," he whispered, "are four men. They will ask you to do something, Johnny, a kind of test and a harsh one at that. If you pass, you will be given over to me for your training."

"What training?" Johnny tried to ask but the big man gently placed a rough finger across his lips.

"No time for questions, boy, not now, but know this, Johnny, if you fail to do what these men ask of you, they will take you far away from here. You will spend the rest of your life in some Godforsaken monastery in the arse end of nowhere. They will bring you up in the faith and make you take vows of silence. They will be kind to you but a prison is a prison, boy, and you will never be allowed to leave. Try not to be afraid, Johnny. I will be with you and I shall pray for you. I can do no more for you now. Come," he said, gently taking his arm. "Let's get this done." The first thing that Johnny noticed as he came through the door was the four men sitting at a square table in the middle of the room. The second thing was the naked man gagged and chained to the wall behind them. For a moment, the world seemed to grow darker and he staggered, only Father Matthew's strong hands keeping him from collapsing. "Stand up," Father Matthew hissed, shaking him roughly. "Now is not the time for weakness."

"It's him," Johnny whimpered. "You don't understand. It's him."

"I know who he is, boy. That's why you are here."

"Enough talk," one of the men at the table said, standing and glaring at Father Matthew. "Is this what you have brought us, Matthew? This boy who whimpers and faints in fear. Is this who you want to apprentice to our sacred cause?"

"Yes," Father Matthew said, stepping in front of Johnny as if to shield him from the other man's gaze. "Yes, I do. I intend to train him and make him my personal apprentice."

"Only if he passes the test," the other man quickly countered.

"And what would you know of test, Roberto. What would you know about any of this? You're nothing more than a glorified clerk, a go between the warriors of God and his holiness, the Pope."

"I am a Cardinal," the other man said, his eyes blazing. "How dare you speak to me that way."

"Now, now," another man said, standing from his position around the table. "No need for such anger. We are all men of God and all of us Cardinals. Father Matthew is more than aware that we are his superiors in rank, if nothing else. Isn't that correct,

Matthew?" For a moment, the two men's eyes locked and a silent message seemed to pass between them. "Of course, your Eminence," Father Matthew said, lowering his gaze. "It has been a long drive and I am not so young as I once was."

"None of us are, my son, none of us are. Well, except this young man," he said, coming from around the table and kneeling before Johnny. "I am Cardinal James Maloy of the most Holy Roman Catholic Church and you are Johnny Masterson. I have heard much about you, Johnny, and know that God has tested you harshly and still more to come." The other men sat at the table suddenly all stood and removed the table and chairs from the centre of the room. As if heeding some silent command, they melted back into the shadows. Yet Johnny could feel their eyes watching. "You know this man don't you, Johnny," the Cardinal said, gently taking his hand and drawing him forward.

"Yes," Johnny whispered, his voice hitching. "He killed my mummy and daddy."

"Yes, yes, he did, Johnny," the Cardinal replied, his voice growing steely. "He has killed lots of mummies and daddies and little children, too. He isn't really a man, Johnny. Do you know what he is?"

"Yes," Johnny replied, wiping angrily at his eyes. "He is a monster."

"That's right, Johnny," the Cardinal said, resting a comforting hand on the boy's shoulder. "He is a monster, a monster that would kill over and over again if we let him, but we're not going to let him. You're not going to let him are you, Johnny?"

"No, not ever again." Johnny was too young to understand the concept of fate or destiny. He only knew when the knife was placed in his hand that it felt right there, and the fear that had engulfed him, smothered him, making it hard to breathe since that terrible night, evaporated, no that wasn't right, it changed, evolved into something else: outrage and white hot desire for revenge.

With a cry of hate, Johnny shook free of the Cardinal and charged at the chained man. The man's eyes widened as he saw the silvered knife and his death fast approaching. He tried to cry out as he strained and heaved against his chains, his huge muscles bunching, but it was too late. The knife slid into his stomach like a hot knife through butter. Johnny screamed as he stabbed the man over and over again, blood splattering his face and wrist, yet the man still would not die. He felt a large hand cover his blood slicked wrist and guide it upwards.

"The heart, Johnny," Father Matthew said from behind him. "Always go for the heart." He did just that, Father Matthew lending him his great strength as together they thrust the blade forward, sliding between bone and piercing the heart within. For a moment, the man's eyes locked on Johnny as if marking him forever then he fell dead to the ground in a bloody heap.

Johnny dropped the knife, clattering to the ground, and groped for Father Matthew who took the sobbing boy in his arms.

"Hate is a seed that grows, Johnny," he whispered in his ear. "You will need that hate. It will sustain you throughout the long years. We will cultivate it together, you and I." That said, he scooped up the young boy and walked past the silent cardinals and out into the future.

That had been over thirty years ago and now Johnny was here hunting what he suspected was the same kind of creature that had so mercilessly destroyed his family. But he was no longer a frightened little boy who had wept uncontrollably after his first kill but an experienced hunter who had destroyed all manner of evil in the name of God. Yet this job unnerved him. There was something wrong with this place. For one thing, it seemed the entire village was deserted.

He had arrived yesterday after receiving a desperate email from a Father Nicholas, the village parish priest, who had awoken in the early hours of the morning to the grisly sight of two dead bodies in his graveyard. Both had been torn up, claw marks defiling their poor broken bodies, sinew and bone gleamed in the early morning light. Both the victims' hearts had been missing. Stuffed in their place, filling the empty cavities, were pages from the Bible both quoting Revelation, "And behold a beast will walk among them!" Father Nicholas had quickly snapped some photos and sent a frantic email to the

Vatican requesting advice. He was told, in no uncertain terms, to remove the bloody pages, to burn them then call the local police and let the authorities take over. Help would be with him soon.

That evening, Johnny Masterson was ordered to the Vatican. There he was briefed on the whole affair, shown the pictures of the two bodies, which he examined closely, taking in the depth and width of the claw marks and the evidence of the missing hearts. He confirmed that the creature involved was most likely a Lycanthrope. From there, he was given the green light and booked on the first available flight to London in the U.K.

He set down at Heathrow airport at six am the following morning, hired a car and headed down south, towards Cornwall.

Five hours later, he was turning into the driveway of St Peter's church. Leaving his bags in the car, he got out then immediately stopped. It suddenly occurred to him that since entering the village he had not seen a single person nor had a single car driven passed him. It was Saturday afternoon and the village was dead silent, not even a bird tweeted in the surrounding trees, nothing. And yet, there was something, a kind of heaviness in the air, an oppression, almost a sense of waiting. Johnny had long ago learned to trust his feelings and something here felt very wrong.

Drawing his gun from his jacket, Johnny flicked off the safety and headed for the church. He had taken no more than a few steps when he noticed the blood on the path. At first, it was nothing more than a few drops but, as he drew closer to the church, it grew thicker, almost covering the entire path. Drag marks ran through it, heading towards the doors that stood open, over the stone steps and into the darkened church beyond.

Johnny squatted down, never taking his eyes off the church doors and dipped an experimental finger into the blood, feeling the texture which was thick, almost jelly like and Johnny guessed the blood was old and already starting to congeal, probably spilled sometime last night while he was still being briefed in Rome.

Standing, he wiped the blood off on his jean clad leg and cocked his weapon before slowly moving towards the door. It was the smell that hit him first, brought to him on a sudden gust of wind that rattled the tree branches all about. It was the smell of death, of flyblown meat crawling with maggots. Johnny covered his nose and mouth with his spare hand, breathing shallowly as he entered the church.

For a moment, he stood there, his hands falling limply to his sides, the smell forgotten as he observed the desecration within. Everywhere there was chaos. Pews were smashed and broken, pages from prayer books and Bibles lay scattered all about. Some of the pages were smeared with a brown substance that could only be either mud or shit but it was the altar that Johnny couldn't look away from. A man's body lay across it, face down, his bloody clothes torn to shreds. His back was also torn, torn right down to the spine. It gleamed wetly, a stark white in a sea of red puckered flesh. Even worse than this, the man whom Johnny guessed correctly was Father Nicholas, had been violated in the worst possible way. From the waist down, he was completely naked, his legs splayed impossibly wide and Johnny presumed they had been dislocated or even broken. His genitals had been torn away and a large brass crucifix had been rammed in their place.

For a moment, the room seemed to spin then the smell hit him again with full force, driving him backwards, surrounding him like a miasma, slicking the back of his throat, making it hard to breathe. Retching, he staggered away, back into blessed daylight. There he was noisily sick, breaking the ominous silence with his retching and heaving.

After he had purged himself, he walked around the desecrated church until he found the rectory. Like the church, the door was open but the inside was untouched and almost barrack neat. Johnny wasted no time and headed straight for the phone. He had his mobile, of course, but there was no signal here, not even a single bar. Likewise, when he checked the priest's phone, there was no dial tone, nothing, just a wall of silence. Cursing, he slammed the phone down and headed back outside. For a moment, he stood there, indecisive, before marching down towards the bottom of the hill.

He had noticed a row of terrace houses on the drive up. He knocked on the door of the first house, noticing the car parked in the drive, but there was no answer. He tried to peer through the curtains but they were shut tight. Heading next door, he rapped on the door, hammered on it, but there was no answer. He peered through the window into a small living room with an oversized T.V but there was nothing, nobody, not even a sullen neighbour asking what the hell all the noise was about.

At the next house, he didn't even bother to knock but just tried the handle. When it didn't turn, he raised one booted foot and kicked it in, wincing as the noise defiled the silence. Inside, he found nothing and that's how it went for the next few hours. In some houses, he found TVs and radios still playing. In another, he found a smoking iron still switched on, which he quickly turned off. In another, a table set for an evening meal, a congealing chicken stew and stale bread sitting on the table. But as for the inhabitants of the village, there was no sign.

By the time he had finished his fruitless searching, it was starting to get dark. For a moment, he considered spending the night in the rectory before starting his search again tomorrow but dismissed the notion quickly. It was too close to the church and the horrors within. Instead, he grabbed his bag out of the car and headed more fully into the village.

He hadn't gone far when he noticed a small hotel just off to his left. The door was open and the lights were on. Maybe someone was home and, if not, at least he would have a place to wait out the night. But after a quick look around, he deduced that this place was just as empty as everywhere else.

Tomorrow he would enter the village and see if he could track down the beast that had killed poor Father Nicholas and, with God's help, maybe find some survivors of whatever had happened in this place.

The next morning he stepped out of the shower intending to do just that. Quickly, he towelled himself dry, threw on yesterday's clothes and armed himself before heading out into the street.

He stood there for a moment, watching and listening, but again there was nothing but the same ominous silence. No people, no birdsong, not so much as a barking dog. Nothing.

He set out walking, digging into his pocket for his mobile phone but the damn thing still had no signal. If he didn't find a way to report soon, the Vatican would send other hunters to find him and that was the last thing that Johnny wanted. There were only five hunters active at the moment, including himself, all working in different locations around the world. The last thing any of them needed was to be pulled off an important job just because Johnny Masterson couldn't find a working phone.

Cursing, he stuffed his mobile back into his pocket then came to an abrupt halt. There was a dead man standing in the middle of the road between the Post Office and the local bakery as if guarding the entrance to the harbour beyond. Johnny unholstered the gun by his side and moved slowly closer. Right now, the creature was looking at the floor, its rotting body swaying in the wind that blew from the ocean beyond. It was impossible to tell what sex the creature had been - it was too far gone into decay for that.

As Johnny drew closer, he noticed bits of seaweed hanging from between blackened ribs and how the top of its balding skull was encrusted with barnacles. He could smell it now. The stench of decaying flesh, rotting seaweed and long dead oceans. Suddenly, the creature's head shot up and it let out a low groan as it staggered towards him, leaving bits of sloughing flesh behind as it came on.

The thing's face was a complete horror. The nose had caved in, leaving two raw channels. The bottom jaw was dislocated and distended, a gaping hole filled with crooked blackened teeth. "Fuck this," Johnny said, raising his pistol and taking a step back. He had dealt with the undead many times before and knew, barring decapitation, a gunshot or extreme trauma to the head was the only way to put them down.

Sighting along his arm, Johnny gently squeezed the trigger. The gun bucked in his hand and the creature's face exploded in a mass of black putrescence. It staggered but did not go down instead continuing its slow advance, arms reaching. Taking a deep breath, Johnny shot off another round, shearing off the top of the creature's head and dropping it in its tracks. He stood still for a moment, smoking gun by his side, eyes searching for anymore movement but there was nothing, only the sighing of the wind and the smell of the ocean.

Flicking on the safety, he holstered his weapon and approached the creature, kneeling by its side, doing his best to ignore the smell. Never in all his years as a hunter had he seen anything like this. Oh, he had seen his fair share of the undead or zombies, if you like, but never anything like this. He wouldn't have believed anything so rotten and decomposed could even move, let alone attack somebody. In most cases of reanimation, it was only the new dead who arose, their empty flesh a vessel for a greater evil, but this thing had been dead for months, maybe even years, a dead fisherman, perhaps, or a victim of accidental drowning. Either way, it had somehow managed to drag itself from its watery grave to try and attack him.

But what was it doing here and what evil had managed to enslave its poor broken body? And was it somehow connected to the murder of Father Nicholas and the mystery of the missing villagers. Nothing made sense. He felt unnerved, almost out of his depth. This was not a clear cut case. This was something else.

Standing, he raised his face to the sky and took a few deep breaths, trying to get his whirling thoughts under control and find a little inner peace. He had a job to do and it wasn't going to get done standing here and second guessing himself.

Straightening, he pulled the shotgun from across his back and continued on past the deserted shops and onto the harbour front. The harbour wasn't one but two, consisting of an inner and outer harbour.

Fishing trawlers of all shapes and sizes bobbed in the murky waters alongside smaller vessels used for crabbing and catching lobster. There was even a small yacht or two, sails furled and tied down against the .coming winter. All about were shops, restaurants, cafes and ice cream parlours, tight closed and bordered over to protect them from the raging sea and winter storm.

He was looking at an ice cream parlour with the unfortunate name of Ice Cream Sea Bream when the second attack came. One minute he was looking up at the swinging sign and in the next his face was hitting the concrete with numbing force as something big and fast barrelled into him from behind. For a second, he just lay there helpless, his body a mass of pain but after what seemed like an age, he managed to stagger to his feet, spitting blood and bits of broken teeth. The shotgun he had been carrying had been knocked from his grasp but lay nearby. Scrambling with reaching fingers, he scooped it up and span around, trying to look everywhere at once.

"Are you looking for me, little chicken?" a voice growled. Johnny turned as if in slow motion. He knew that voice. It was a voice he would never forget, the voice that still haunted his dreams. The creature that had killed his parents, the creature that he himself had killed so many years ago, was crouched down on a nearby boat that bobbed and rocked in the growing wind, its malevolent eyes never leaving his face.

"Oh Johnny," it growled creeping forward, "how you have grown." It was closer now, only an inch or two of water between them and Johnny fancied he could smell its fetid breath. "What's the matter, Johnny," the thing crooned. "Aren't you going to piss your pants for me again?"

"No," Johnny replied, raising the shotgun to the creature's face. "No, I'm not." The creature continued to smile as Johnny pulled the trigger, emptying both barrels into its face at point blank range, dissolving its head in an explosion of blood, teeth and bone. For a moment, it lay there twitching then lay still.

Quickly, Johnny reloaded his weapon then leapt across the churning sea and onto the rocking boat, but the creature was gone. There was nothing. No blood, no body, nothing.

Suddenly, he heard laughter from behind him, the high sweet laughter of a child, and spun around, almost falling over the little girl that had seemingly materialised out of nowhere. The girl could have been no older than five, maybe six. She was dressed in a simple white nightgown that was streaked with dirt and blood. Her hair was a mass of black tangles, her face filthy.

"I didn't give you permission to come aboard," she said, smiling sweetly. Johnny was just about to stutter out a reply when her hand shot out, grabbing him by the balls. She hoisted him into the air and over the side into the freezing cold water below. For a moment, Johnny was falling, the pain in his balls a white hot fire, until he hit the water, its cold embrace stealing his breath, almost stopping his heart. Spluttering and gasping, he broke the surface and swam for a nearby ladder that led out of the churning sea and back onto the harbour side.

Grasping the ladder, he hoisted himself out of the freezing cold water and just stopped. There was a pile of bodies on the quayside, not a pile but a hill, a mountain of lolling dead bodies. All the missing people from the village, men, women and children slaughtered. Hundreds of them, thousands, and, sat atop this macabre throne, the same little girl that had so easily vanquished him only a moment ago.

"Hello, Johnny. We're so glad you could make it."

"Who are you? What are you and why have you done this?"

"Me?" she said, smiling sweetly.

"Yes, you," Johnny said, his anger growing until it burned like a hot rock in the pit of his stomach. "You are behind all this. All the rest was just an illusion."

"How clever you are, Johnny, how innocent and how little you know, how little they have told you." Johnny's rage and frustration overcame him then and he slapped leather. Drawing his guns, he fired into the murderous thing above him, emptying both clips into this thing masquerading as a child, but the guns had no effect, passing through the creature as if passing through a haze of smoke.

"Now, now, Johnny," it chuckled. "Violence begets violence." Suddenly, the guns in his hands glowed white hot and he dropped them with a cry, his hands blistering and weeping as he gritted his teeth against the pain. "Those little toys of yours can't hurt me, Johnny," it said, toying with a dead woman's hair. "But you asked who I am and why I have done this. The answer to your first question is that I am a messenger and as to why? My master wanted to attract your attention, Johnny. He has chosen you to deliver a message to your dog masters in Rome."

"Message?" Johnny frowned. "What message and who in God's name is your master?" All of a sudden she was there before him floating, levitating, surrounded by a stinking haze of smoking sulphur and reeking flies. She grabbed him by the throat, spun him around and thrust him face first into the pile of rotting bodies.

"Look upon me and despair," she hissed from between rotting teeth, her eyes glowing crimson orbs in her face. "I am darkness, fear and hate. My master is the morning star, the master of flies, the dark one, motherfucking Lucifer. Is that clear to you now, Johnny? Does that compute? Answer me," she screeched, shaking him back and forth like a terrier with a rat. "Answer me you Bible thumping Jesus loving fuck. Answer me!" But Johnny could not. His vision was fading, his hearing going far away.

Suddenly, the choking hand around his throat was gone and he staggered away, holding his throat. Gasping for breath, he heaved then fell to his knees, vomiting a mixture of bile and blood onto the floor, the stink of the dead all over him.

"Forgive me, Johnny," the creature tittered now, sitting back atop her grisly throne. "Sometimes my temper gets the best of me. Do I have your attention now?" she said as Johnny staggered back to his feet.

"Fuck you," he spat at her. For a moment, she just sat there, a look of stunned surprise upon her face, before bursting out into a deep rumbling laughter.

"I like you, Johnny. You have balls. Perhaps I will tear them off and wear them as earrings, after all you don't need your balls to deliver a message now, do you."

"What message?" Johnny gasped, wincing at the pain in his throat.

"Very well," she said, climbing to her feet. "No more games. From my master's lips to your ears. My master, Lucifer, commands me to tell your masters in Rome the first prophecy has been fulfilled. The end of days is upon them. Look for star Wormwood in the sky and prepare to drink of bitter waters. The pit shall be opened and the hordes of hell shall run free upon your lands. We're coming, Johnny," she said, starting down towards him, sending bodies tumbling like broken dolls. "Tell them," she said, beginning to change and grow, her skin turning black and peeling, starting to smoke. Now she reared above him, black wings bursting from her back, a haze of intense heat beating against him, blistering his skin as he turned to flee.

"She is alive, Johnny," she shrieked after him. "Your mother. They lied to you, Johnny. She is alive. She runs with the moon and eats the flesh of the innocent. She will be waiting for you, Johnny. I will give her your regards. Tell them, Johnny. Tell them what I said. My master is coming, coming for them, coming for you, Johnny!" Its voice reverberated around the village, shattering windows, causing blood to flow between his fingers where he clamped them desperately to his head as he ran into a future of pain and destruction where the minions of hell stalked the earth and hope, like redemption, was a long forgotten dream.

Broken Messiah, the novel, coming soon.

Printed in Poland
by Amazon Fulfillment
Poland Sp. z o.o., Wrocław